DEATH-RUSH

The jungle had become unusually quiet.

McLeane mounted his silencer, then heard the clear tread of boots through the brush coming toward him. The Japs had sent their noisiest troops to keep Hill 457, McLeane thought to himself. He supported his .45 across his left arm, pointed it ahead, and waited.

Soon the footsteps stopped.

McLeane continued to wait.

Nothing happened.

Suddenly, an excruciating pain shot up his right arm as a Jap boot came down hard on his hand. Another Jap rushed him from the side.

McLeane wanted to scream. Instead, he grabbed his carbine and unloaded it into the Jap who was rushing him. The man didn't know what hit him.

From above, the dead Jap's friend fired his Nambu at point-blank range. McLeane felt bullets fly past his face. One grazed his right cheek and blood rolled onto his upper lip.

McLeane spun away, taking his would-be killer out with a kick to the knees and falling back onto the dead soldier. Blood poured out of the dead soldier's body. For an instant McLeane fogged over. In that long moment McLeane found himself face-to-face with what, in the dark, looked like a sword. . . .

NEW ADVENTURES FROM ZEBRA!

McLEANE'S RANGERS #3

HELL ON HILL 457

BY JOHN DARBY

ZEBRA BOOKS
KENSINGTON PUBLISHING CORP.

ZEBRA BOOKS

are published by

KENSINGTON PUBLISHING CORP.
475 Park Avenue South
New York, N.Y. 10016

First printing: March, 1984

Printed in the United States of America

One

McLeane had the Rangers working out. Wilkins and O'Connor spent most of the day running around Vella la Vella. They were sweating bullets as they made another pass by McLeane.

"How many's that?" he yelled.

Wilkins shrugged to say he didn't know, turned, and jogged backward for a while. O'Connor, the sweat dripping down his face and built more for smashing brick walls than double-timing in sand anyway, gestured unmistakably with his middle finger.

McLeane smiled.

Directly in front of him, under a relentless tropical sun, Contardo and Heinman each tried to do more push-ups than the other. On the soft, grainy ground of the Solomon Islands that had to be hard.

"One hundred twenty-one," Contardo shouted,

smug in the fact that he remained two ahead of Heinman.

McLeane felt reassured. He had the best fighters anywhere on his side. Categorically no one handled small arms half as well as Wilkins. Gunning squirrels in the Georgia woods had taught him more about weapons than all the ordinance officers in all the services ever learned in school. Last time out Wilkins nailed a scorpion a hair from Contardo's nose. McLeane grinned. Contardo stayed angry for two days because the bullet ripped a hole in the tent.

As for Contardo, McLeane considered him the biggest pain-in-the-ass and the most courageous trooper he had ever seen. Nobody took him in hand-to-hand combat. Against an angry grizzly, McLeane would put his money on Contardo. Contardo had the instincts as well as the personality of a panther and a dedication to the Rangers and the Brooklyn Dodgers that, in the end, would leave him mindlessly fighting the entire Japanese army single-handedly in order to save someone's neck or win a pennant.

O'Connor built bombs for all occasions. How he'd learned to do that as a Chicago bartender McLeane never did learn. But he could blow up half a mountain with something the size of a pocket watch just as easily as he could detonate a fly on the back of a general's hand fifty miles away. McLeane also did not forget O'Connor's ham-hock fists which he used to paralyze people.

"One hundred thirty-eight," shouted Contardo.

"One hundred thirty-seven," answered Heinman.

Heinman had closed the gap by one.

Of all the Rangers he had to be the most accomplished. As a karate expert, a linguist and oriental scholar, and an American who had studied at Oxford, only McLeane really understood him. The others liked him well enough; he had bailed them out more than once either by breaking a Jap's neck or sweet-talking some hungry native out of eating one of them. And despite their bickering, Contardo and he had a special rapport. In the end, though, McLeane came closest to being like Heinman. They shared academic interests and liked to talk. But with a war on who had time to talk?

O'Connor and Wilkins had disappeared somewhere around the island. McLeane looked again at Contardo and Heinman.

"One hundred forty-four."

They sounded almost together.

By 1700 everyone had had enough. Contardo and Heinman ended their contest in a dead tie which did not keep Contardo from insisting that he'd won. Wilkins felt just great, or so he said, and O'Connor complained about losing five pounds.

"Now my pants don't fit," he grumbled, holding them gathered at the waist with one hand.

"It's the latest fashion," McLeane assured him.

"What's all this physical training about anyway, sir?" Heinman asked. "It's not like we don't work out. We're all in pretty good shape."

"General's orders."

"That's it? General's orders."

"That's it. Now get something to eat."

The Rangers headed back to the mess. McLeane turned and took long, quick strides across the clearing bordered by banyan trees and areca palms, to where Margot waited for him with, he hoped, something to eat.

No, he knew nothing more about the extended physical training program than what General Thompson had told him, that the men had to be in top condition even if it meant running them day and night. He did not know either what had been bothering Margot for the last couple of days.

An iron crossbar had been erected at the entrance to his tent. McLeane grabbed hold with one hand and chinned himself fifty times.

"Eight minutes, twenty seconds," he muttered to himself. "No good."

His shirt, soaked through with sweat, clung to him like skin.

He went inside.

Margot had outdone herself with the dinner. Instead of fresh bonito or albacore, for which McLeane always gladly settled, she treated him to New Zealand leg of lamb with mint jelly, fresh broccoli, real potatoes, and a salad made from greens less than a week old. This he washed down with a Pouilly-Fuissé 1938 that he chased, after dinner, with Remy Martin. The presence of the wine and the cognac on the table gave McLeane cause to wonder, as did Margot's solicitous attitude throughout the entire evening. McLeane held a real cup filled with genuine American coffee in his hand and tried to understand the reason for the last couple of hours.

Sitting across from him, Margot looked absolutely ravishing. She had let her bright red hair fall down around her shoulders, had tucked in her long, shapely legs. The top three buttons on her blouse had opened, revealing a cleavage McLeane could see from the other side of the room. Could she really be in the Marine Corps, McLeane asked himself, and a radio specialist at that?

"Great dinner, Margot."

"Glad you liked it." Margot nodded and smiled.

"I especially liked the New Zealand lamb." McLeane swirled the coffee in its cup. "That's the part of the meal I especially liked."

"I thought you would," she said, smiling.

"I also liked the wine, babe, and the Remy."

"I *knew* you would." Margot had not stopped smiling from the moment she had put dinner on the table.

McLeane waited.

"Where did they come from, Margot?"

"What, dear?"

McLeane hated games.

"The lamb, the Pouilly-Fuissé, the Remy, the fresh broccoli, the real potatoes." He held up his cup. "This coffee."

"Oh, those. The coffee and everything."

"Yeah."

"They came from General Thompson," Margot said matter-of-factly.

"I thought so," McLeane shook his head slowly up and down. "Why do you suppose he wanted me to eat so well?"

"I don't know, but in a few minutes you can ask him."

Suddenly, McLeane had a better reading of Margot's smile, the smile she had pasted on her face since he had walked in the door.

They sat without saying anything. Before long both of them heard a jeep pull up outside. Margot stood up, buttoned her blouse, and straightened her skirt. McLeane looked hard at her long red hair; at her breasts, soft and firm; at her hips and legs and knew, in that moment, that only she could be his girl and a marine to boot.

"You're out of uniform, Corporal," he said and pointed to her shoes which she slipped on hurriedly.

"Come in, sir," McLeane called as he walked to the door.

A gaunt, fiftyish man with closely cropped gray hair entered the tent. Normally someone who wore the pain of stomach ulcers on his face, General Thompson relaxed his eyebrows and smiled long enough to greet McLeane and Margot.

"Hello, Mack," he said, shaking hands. "Hello, Margot. You look lovely."

"Would you like a glass of Remy Martin, sir?" McLeane asked. "Margot happened to find some today. Or, if you haven't already eaten, I'm sure there's a little lamb, New Zealand lamb, left . . . with fresh broccoli. Unfortunately, the Pouilly-Fuissé, 1938, is all gone, but—"

"I know, Mack," the general smiled. "What's this all about, right?"

"Right."

The two of them sat down and Margot poured a

round of cognac.

"I can't tell you everything." The general's eyebrows came together again. "This much, however, you must know. You and your men will be heading out on your most dangerous mission yet. For that mission you will all need intensive parachute training."

"Sounds ominous, sir. What did I just eat? My last full meal?"

The general chuckled. "I wanted you to feel good when we talked."

McLeane looked off for a long moment. He did not like mysteries when they involved him. What would he tell the men? "Listen up! We're going back to jump school to prepare for a mission about which I know nothing except that none of us may make it." That ought to put them at ease.

"Mack, trust me on this." The general spoke in his best trust-me-on-this voice.

"I do, sir." McLeane did his best to sound sincere.

Suddenly, Margot got up and, excusing herself, left the tent, closing the flap just a little too hard behind her.

McLeane apologized.

"I'm sorry about that, sir."

"Oh, she's known about this for a couple of days already."

"She isn't happy."

"She cares about you."

"I care about me, too. I also care about four guys who ought to get some breaks in this war."

"I understand," said General Thompson reassur-

11

ingly. "And believe me intelligence has done a superb job on this one."

"Intelligence is Major Flagg, isn't it?" McLeane knew the answer before he asked the question.

"I know how you feel about Major Flagg, Mack. But he has outdone himself this time."

How could anyone tell? McLeane thought to himself. What a stupid, pompous ass! Flagg could best help the Americans by fighting for Japan.

General Thompson stood to leave. McLeane walked him to the door. They shook hands.

"Corrigan will fly you out at 1700 tomorrow, Mack."

Maybe Corrigan was arrogant, but he knew how to fight. McLeane could set his watch by him. He smiled.

"I thought you'd like that," General Thompson replied to McLeane's obvious lift in spirits.

"I'm not sure *like* is the word, sir."

The general disappeared out the door.

McLeane had needed air.

When he returned from a quick walk around the camp at Vella la Vella he found Margot, the Redbird, marine and radio specialist, flung across the bed, sobbing. He sat next to her and stroked her hair.

"Do you love me?" she asked, lifting her head.

McLeane took pride in always being truthful. Certainly, he loved no one else more.

"Yes," he said simply, though he wondered how the question related to the war effort generally and the campaign in the Pacific specifically.

He lay down beside her.

"What's wrong?" he asked tenderly.

"It's the same. It's always the same." She cried into a pillow. "You're never here long enough for us to be together. Two weeks, three weeks and off you go again. And each time it's worse than the last."

She paused and looked him in the eye.

"Someday you're going to get killed."

Actually, that thought had never bothered him. Maybe he never really took the possibility seriously. After a while the physical strain of the mission would begin to get to him. After a while he always just wanted to come home. But he never really considered dying.

"What are you supposed to do, anyway?" Margot shouted, slamming her fist on the bed. "Win the whole fucking war by yourself?"

McLeane had wondered about that himself. He did feel sometimes that he and the Rangers were the only ones out there. At the moment, however, Margot had gotten to him. He had never heard her use that kind of language.

"Hey, sweetheart, take it easy." He talked softly and tried to gentle her. They lay together without saying anything for a while.

"And I hate the way Thompson made me part of it this time." Margot had not quite finished her agenda. McLeane kissed her hair, rubbed her back.

"Come on," he said. "I'll put you to bed." He held her tightly in his arms.

"I love you, Mack."

Margot rolled over and searched McLeane's face

for some kind of affirmation.

Again McLeane said he loved her. Years ago he'd learned that women never tire of hearing those words. He said them one more time as he slowly unbuttoned her blouse. He felt her breasts heave under his hand. Deftly, he removed her bra, buried his face in her warm flesh, and said once again how much he loved her. He kissed her nipples, eyes, and mouth.

"You do love me, Mack. I know you love me."

She pulled her skirt off over her hips and slipped out of her panties.

McLeane kissed her belly.

Margot tore at his shirt and then grabbed at his belt.

"Easy, easy," McLeane quieted her.

"I want you."

McLeane flung aside his shirt that night without the usual regard for insect life on Vella la Vella. The mosquitoes could drain them both of blood for all he cared.

Margot, in hungry anticipation gyrating on the bed, murmured, "Please" as her hands caressed her own body.

In a moment they were twined together.

"Please let me, let me, Mack." And Margot moved to touch his loins with her lips. She swore to herself right there that she would always and forever love him with her mouth, all of her body, with everything she had.

An eternity passed before McLeane gently lowered her to the bed. He kissed her all over, lingering between her thighs.

"Please, please."

Margot pulled McLeane on top of her.

"Now, Mack, please now."

McLeane held her arms over her head, smiled and, without making a sound, formed the word *no* with his lips.

His body touched hers ever so lightly.

"Please, please." She spoke in a voice barely audible and ground her hips into the bed. The more she begged the more he tormented her. The more he tormented her, the more she begged.

Then he entered her when she least expected him and they moved together until their passion became unbearable.

Suddenly, Margot grabbed his body hard with her legs.

"I love you," she screamed.

McLeane held her tightly, buried his head in her neck. Then they both fell limp.

McLeane could hear her sobbing beneath him, feel her move in quiet throbs. He waited and rolled to her side.

"Are you all right?" he asked.

"I've never felt better," she said laughing between the sobs. She snuggled next to him. He put his arm around her and looked at the ceiling. Soon he felt her body move in the slow even rhythm of sleep. He looked over at her and wondered where Thompson would send him next.

Two

Seventy-three and three-eighths miles southwest of Vella La Vella, where the eighth latitude crosses the one hundred fifty-fifth longitude, lies a plot of land so small most maps don't show it. The Rangers decided to call it Lonelyville. There, General Thompson had erected a special parachuting facility and there, for no one knew how long, the Rangers would practice jumping out of a plane onto a dime.

Not even Corrigan felt good about the idea as the Catalina flew the Rangers toward their destination.

"I hate to say it, McLeane, but this time I almost feel sorry for you." Corrigan's voice sounded something like sincere as he piloted his broken-down seaplane over nothing but water.

Farther back in the plane Contardo turned to Heinman. "I bet there's nothing but water under us."

"Did you figure that out all by yourself?"

Contardo had long ago established his lack of faith in aeronautical science. Ever since Heinman had explained how high speed created a vacuum above the wing and how this vacuum allowed the push of air below the wing to keep the plane afloat, Contardo had declared himself a devout skeptic concerning all things not firmly fastened to the ground. As for the Catalina, he believed each flight would be his last.

"Nope, I'm glad I'm not in your shoes," Corrigan continued to McLeane.

"Spare me, Corrigan. You're in this as much as we are." With Corrigan, McLeane always felt a periodic need to reestablish the relationship.

"I'll tell you this, McLeane," Corrigan said, his Australian accent taking on a sinister tone. "Anything happen to my baby here and I'll take care of you myself."

He gave the instrument panel a pat.

"And another thing. I ain't saving your ass no more." He leaned toward McLeane. "You get your ass in trouble. You get it out. Still leaning toward McLeane, he added, "And something else I want to tell you—"

McLeane cut him short.

"Better keep your eyes on the road, Corrigan. That time you almost ran over a kangaroo."

Corrigan kept looking straight ahead.

"Fuck you, McLeane."

McLeane smiled.

"Good to be working with you again, Corrigan."

For the remainder of the short flight they did not speak much except to check their bearings.

Lonelyville proved to be everything the Rangers expected and less.

They waded in from just off shore to be greeted by an Army master sergeant and a tech sergeant.

"Major, sir, my name is Fuqua, and this is Tech Sergeant Barlow. We've been expecting you."

The men shook hands all around. Corrigan had anchored the Catalina. McLeane pointed to him jumping into the water.

"The dapper gentleman with, as you will soon notice, a thin mustache is Corrigan. He is Australian, which is why he sounds funny when he talks, has a rotten personality, but, and this is important, knows what he's doing. Don't tell him I said that. Otherwise, there is absolutely no reason to pay any attention to him at all."

"That's not quite right, sir, but I'll explain all that later," Sergeant Fuqua replied cryptically. "First, let me explain what you will all be doing here."

"Ain't you gonna show us around?" Contardo asked.

Everyone laughed.

"I'm afraid this is it, Sergeant," Fuqua responded. "Except for a few rocks on the other side of that swamp grass over there this is as fancy as it gets."

O'Connor wanted to know who made the Army in charge instead of the Marines, but decided to save the question.

"While we're all together, let me just explain that I was sent here from Fort Bragg on this special assignment. I don't know any more about it than you do and probably less. I don't know why anybody chose me for the job, but here I am. If it makes you feel any better, I was a jump instructor before this war started. I've thrown myself out of a plane three hundred fifty-two times which may be a record. All my time in the service I've been with the 101st, and, no offense, but I wish I was with them now, frankly."

O'Connor noticed the Screaming Eagle on the sergeant's shoulder. Everyone had heard of the 101st. Fuqua looked all right, was built a little like O'Connor himself. Still, O'Connor would have felt better if he had been a marine. He decided to ignore the other sergeant, Barlow, altogether. A patch of land as small as Lonelyville had room for only one dogface at a time.

"I only want to show you one thing here on the island." They all followed Sergeant Fuqua to a cluster of especially tall banyan trees.

"Most banyan trees are about one hundred fifty feet high," Fuqua said. "These, however, are almost twice that size."

Everyone looked up.

"In fact," continued the sergeant, "they are almost the exact size of a regulation jump tower. We have it rigged so you can begin target practice from up there. We won't have to camouflage anything that way. When you get good from there, we can move to the plane."

The Rangers could see wires leading up to what

looked like a platform high above them, and wooden rungs had been fastened onto the trees. Heinman grabbed one of the rungs hard.

"They're secure, Lieutenant," Sergeant Fuqua reassured him. "The engineers put them up—the Army engineers."

Everyone except O'Connor laughed.

"Besides, I've taken a few jumps myself already," continued Sergeant Fuqua. "I don't think there's too much else to say except that you bivouac wherever you're comfortable, and we begin in the morning."

During the briefing, Corrigan had brought what looked like supplies onto the island. He stopped to talk privately to the two Army sergeants and then headed back to the Catalina.

"Where's he going?" O'Connor asked with irritation. Dealing with the Army would require a period of adjustment for O'Connor.

"Who? Corrigan?"

"Who else?"

"Oh, don't worry about him," said Sergeant Fuqua.

"I'm not worried about him. I want to know where he's going."

"Back to Vella La Vella, I guess. But he'll be back."

O'Connor displayed clear signs of a man annoyed with life at that moment.

"What's wrong, O'Connor?" Wilkins asked.

"I don't know," replied O'Connor, walking away from the group. "I don't like missions I don't know nothing about. I don't like being in places that ain't on the map." He said nothing about being around the Army.

"Leave him alone," said McLeane.

Heinman raised his hand.

"Yes, Lieutenant?" Fuqua said.

"What did you mean, Sergeant, when you said that Corrigan would be back?"

"Only that he'll be flying the plane you'll all be jumping out of when the time comes."

The Catalina's engines started up.

McLeane imagined Corrigan sitting at the instrument panel grinning from ear to ear. He even found himself smiling.

That evening the Rangers bivouacked as far apart as possible. The summer sun takes a long time going down in that part of the Pacific, but the men just lay around.

Heinman sat propped against a banyan tree writing a letter. O'Connor looked up at the sky and tried to remember how falling out of a plane felt. He did not recall the experience as one of his favorites. In fact, on his last jump, he thought he kept his eyes closed all the way down.

"Fuck it," he said out loud and tried to fall asleep.

On a blanket before him Wilkins had spread all the parts to the Nambu automatic he'd found on the Ranger's last urgent visit to the enemy-held island, New Britain. The piece was a 7mm, a handy enough weapon. He spent the remaining couple of hours of half-light putting the gun back together. He found the design very interesting but the cartridge ineffective. A short-recoil-operated arm locked by a cam coming up from below. The receiver will jam as many times as it won't, Wilkins thought to himself.

"Japs ain't going to win the war with the piece of shit," he said to no one in particular. He patted his conventional Smith & Wesson 9-mm auto pistol at his side. The Japs couldn't learn to make anything that good if they went to school forever.

McLeane chain-smoked Chesterfields and stared off into the Pacific. Directly in front of him lay Bougainville; to his right, northeast on the map, Choiseul. He had just come from Vella La Vella, also to the northeast. He couldn't imagine why the Rangers would be needed for anything southeast, south, or east. Bougainville always remained a possibility The Huon peninsula sat on his left. MacArthur had a lot of troops out there.

He lit another Chesterfield. The only exercise more futile than trying to fight the war was trying to second-guess it. Besides, who told him anything anyway? Did the generals consult him before they got into trouble? Did Thompson ever call to ask advice on how stupid he could be? No, they always waited until after a division found itself lost in a cave or was wiped out trying to take a volcano. McLeane threw the Chesterfield into the sand and lit another one. At least he couldn't hear Margot crying anymore.

O'Connor's voice broke the silence.

"You know what I don't hear?"

No one replied.

"I don't hear someone's fat guinea mouth going."

Contardo had become conspicuous by his silence. He just lay on his bedroll close to where the ocean lapped onto the beach, unsheltered, and said nothing.

"Hey, Contardo, you alive?"

After a long moment, O'Connor called out again. "Hey, Ginzo, you all right?"

When he heard no answer, O'Connor began to get up.

"Leave him," McLeane said without so much as looking back.

"But maybe he's sick," O'Connor suggested.

"He can take care of himself."

O'Connor settled down again to look at the sky.

A few minutes later McLeane walked over to where Contardo lay on his side staring out at the sea.

"You O.K., Contardo?" McLeane asked.

"Yes, sir," said Contardo without moving.

"Take care of yourself," said McLeane as he turned away.

Contardo's knees came up under his chin and he wrapped his arms around himself. McLeane noticed he had on his fatigue cap.

The same sun that sets late in the Solomons also rises early. The Rangers broke camp with the first light. Even before that Sergeants Fuqua and Barlow had made a brew resembling coffee and something like small spheres of dough they claimed to be biscuits. The Rangers ate breakfast with one eye on the jump tower.

Every Ranger jumps. Jumping comes with the

job. Some Rangers more than others like throwing themselves off high places and out of planes. All of them do it.

"You're all accomplished paratroopers," Sergeant Fuqua said, getting the day started. "The only difference between what we're going to do now and anything you've done before is the accuracy with which you've done it."

He walked over to the jump tower improvised from banyan trees. He indicated a circle five feet in diameter, made of stones, directly below the platform.

"The exercise, gentlemen, is to drop into this circle. Remember, you gain control over the chute by manipulating the straps."

Sergeant Fuqua demonstrated.

Heinman couldn't wait.

"Don't forget to hook onto the guide wires going up," Sergeant Fuqua cautioned. Barlow helped the men into their gear.

McLeane got first shot. He floated down smiling right into the center of the circle. Heinman followed with the same look on his face, but not quite with the same accuracy.

"That's all right, sir," said Sergeant Fuqua. "We are going to have many opportunities to practice."

Wilkins took a while longer on the platform. Finally, he missed the target by too much.

"The straps," he grumbled. "I never know which one to pull." He walked away annoyed with himself.

O'Connor never pretended to be a jumper. He

took his time before he dropped. Cursing all the way down, he finally reached the ground, but too far away from the circle.

Contardo waited his turn. He climbed the tree slowly. Once on the platform he froze.

Sergeant Fuqua called up to him.

"Just step off. The guide wires have you."

Nothing worked.

"What's the problem, Major, sir?" Sergeant Fuqua asked McLeane.

"I really don't know," McLeane answered looking up at the figure on the platform.

After a while, Heinman volunteered to go up and find out if Contardo needed help. At once, he rejected his own suggestion.

"You're right," he said to McLeane, correcting himself. "He'd probably shoot me."

"Probably," agreed McLeane.

"Sir, we can't wait much longer, and I'm a little worried," said Sergeant Fuqua. "I'm sending Sergeant Barlow up . . . unless you have some other idea."

"My other idea is to wait, Sergeant, but this is your playground. I just want you to know that I'm not responsible for whatever happens to Sergeant Barlow."

Sergeant Barlow scurried up the tree like a native.

"Where's he going?" O'Connor wanted to know.

No one answered. O'Connor did not want any dogface helping out a marine. Soldiers only made good clerk typists and most of the time not even that. Wisely, he kept this opinion to himself.

In no time Sergeant Barlow had reached the top of the jump tower. From the ground the men could see two figures on the platform, but could hear nothing.

"What's going on?"

O'Connor had slipped deeply into one of his aggravated moods. From past experience McLeane knew that weeks could go by before he got back to normal. This parachuting had set the big Irishman off his stride. The Army's presence did not help either.

The Rangers with Sergeant Fuqua waited.

Then they saw a parachute open and Sergeant Barlow drift down. He hit the circle in dead center.

"Well," Sergeant Barlow said extracting himself from his chute. "He's up there."

"What did he say? What's wrong?"

Sergeant Fuqua seemed concerned.

"What's wrong?" Sergeant Barlow repeated. "I think he's scared . . . only I wouldn't tell him that. What did he say? You don't want to know what he said."

"What did he say?"

"He said that if I didn't get the fuck out of his way he would blow my fucking ass out of the fucking tree."

McLeane nodded his head in recognition.

"You talked to the right guy. That's for sure."

For a brief moment O'Connor smiled.

Suddenly a parachute opened at the top of the tower.

"Shit," Sergeant Fuqua said under his breath. "It opened too soon."

Contardo drifted down slowly along the guidelines. By the time he landed, well outside the circle, his otherwise swarthy, Mediterranean complexion had taken on the same color as the parachute. He stood there stunned for an instant; then a slight breeze off the ocean took the chute and started to pull him. Sergeant Barlow went to lend a hand.

"Get the fuck away from me."

Unaided, Contardo managed to get himself tangled in all the straps and lines. He spent the next ten minutes cursing. Everyone else laughed. Contardo managed to call each one of them, along with the Japanese, General Thompson, and Franklin Delano Roosevelt, every name in his repertoire.

"He has a sweet disposition, doesn't he, sir," Sergeant Fuqua remarked to McLeane.

"The kind we're looking for," McLeane answered. "To get this job, you've got to flunk the personality test."

"Somebody get me out of this fucking thing," Contardo finally yelled.

O'Connor and Heinman went over to him.

"Can't you do anything right?" O'Connor asked, enjoying himself for the first time in days.

"Shut the fuck up."

"I think we should leave him like this, don't you, O'Connor?" Heinman suggested.

"Till the war's over."

"I'll kill both of you."

"See how he talks to people who help him." O'Connor held the chute while Heinman got him loose. "I've noticed, Contardo, that you are not a very nice person."

"I'll kick your ass when I get out of here."

28

McLeane decided this was as good a time as any, and better than most, to find out what had happened on the platform.

"What happened up there, Contardo?"

"Nothing, sir."

"I know that. Why did nothing happen?"

"I guess I got scared, sir."

No one said anything. The Rangers had a great respect for fear. McLeane nodded in understanding. Contardo removed himself from the tangle of lines and straps. He heaved a sigh of relief and wiped his palms along the sides of his pants. Suddenly, he got very serious.

"You see, sir," he said looking directly at McLeane, "I never jumped before."

McLeane let that one sink in a moment.

"You never jumped before."

"No, sir, I'm afraid of heights."

"So am I," volunteered O'Connor. "But you've got to jump. All Rangers got to jump. You can't be a Ranger unless you jump."

"He's right, Contardo," said McLeane. "And you know that."

"Yeah, well you see I had my Ranger training interrupted when my Dad died. I went home for a couple of weeks. When I came back, my class was finishing jump school. They wanted to recycle me, but I paid off some clerk typist to forge my record to make it look like I had already been airborne. I lay low and picked up my class after all that jumping stuff was over. Nobody said nothing."

"Where did you do your Ranger training?" O'Connor asked Fuqua.

"Fort Ord."

The Army, O'Connor thought to himself. A bunch of candyasses. Clerk typists. None of that shit would have happened at Pendleton.

"Well, Sergeant," Fuqua said to Contardo, "we've got a lot of work to catch up on."

Without a word Contardo walked over to the rungs leading to the top of the jump tower.

Three

Maj. Gen. Noboru Sasaki had full responsibility for the Japanese effort in that part of the Pacific around the Solomon Islands and the Bismarck Archipelago, including New Britain and New Guinea. During the summer of 1943, he realized that that effort had slowed down and all but died. Put another way, the effort needed more effort.

A good deal of the problem had to do with military tactics, logistics, equipment, and morale—the usual aspects of war that demoralize and have demoralized all armies since the beginning of war.

But some of the problem also had to do with five marines who had the habit of showing up when least expected and when, from the Japanese viewpoint, least appreciated. Sasaki had come to know them as McLeane's Rangers, and he did not like them.

General Sasaki did not like them for three reasons. First, they took a lot of effort out of the effort he was directing. Second, they made his particular troops look particularly bad. After the Rangers killed 500 soldiers at Rabaul, 100 Japanese for every marine, the general had much to explain to the Emperor. Third, they occupied his time when he would rather have been off establishing military policy with the Japanese chiefs of staff, planning clever tactical maneuvers that would go down in history, and drinking expensive saki in fancy geisha houses back in Tokyo and Kyoto. On balance, Mc-Leane's Rangers had become for him what his American counterpart in Vella La Vella would have called a pain in the ass.

The general decided to treat this pain by passing it on to Maj. Jinichi Imamura, a crack commando attached to the Eighth Combined Special Naval Landing Force. He had chosen Major Imamura not only because of his reputation as a brilliant and courageous soldier but also on the basis of his education. Imamura had studied chemistry at Princeton, knew English fluently, and had an intimate knowledge of the American people and their customs.

Imamura arrived within hours of being summoned to Sasaki's hideaway in the Finnisterre Mountains on the Huon peninsula. There, the general unceremoniously briefed the major on his mission. That mission amounted to "getting rid of these Rangers fast and forever." The general, clearly annoyed at having to spend time on such a trivial matter, handed several folders to Imamura with the proviso that he be successful or else and then left the room, his boots pounding angrily on the hardwood floor.

Imamura made sure Sasaki had left before he plopped himself into the large easy chair by the window and crossed his legs Western style. The major had a great deal of respect for the general's reputation as a formidable military man, tough, but fair with his troops. A generation separated them, however, and Sasaki's old-world Eastern ways, at best, got on Imamura's nerves. He lit a Chesterfield and settled back to read the folders in front of him.

McLeane, of course, interested him most. Japanese Intelligence had quite a bit of information on him. From the picture he looked very all-American, blond, square-jawed, blue-eyed. At six feet two inches he stood five inches over Imamura who counted himself among the taller Japanese. McLeane weighed about 185 pounds, had demonstrated ability as as ace marksman, and was an expert in martial arts and a knowledgeable orientalist. Most of all, however, Japanese Intelligence had found his intelligence was his main asset as a marine; the greatest danger he posed to an enemy lay in his ability to size up situations quickly and to solve problems imaginatively and on the spot. Those qualities Imamura respected as being very American. Intelligence also noted that McLeane had the full respect of his men as well as the love of a woman named Margot. At the mention of her name the report referred to another folder. That, however, did not interest Imamura whose eyes lingered on an earlier bit of information.

"So he went to Columbia," Imamura said to

himself in perfect English, "took liberal arts, played football, and spent a year studying international affairs."

Imamura felt reassured. Roosevelt had gone to Harvard. America seemed determined to keep the war within the Ivy League. He also wondered if the Americans put as much bullshit in their intelligence reports as the Japanese.

Corrigan had not had such a good time since the war started. Flying the Rangers over Lonelyville, watching them fall out of the Catalina, curse, go back, and do it again and again until they dropped perfectly inside a circle so small he could barely see it from 750 feet did his heart good. Contardo, especially, gave him a laugh. Sergeant Fuqua may have taught the loudest marine in the war how to jump, but no one would ever make him like it. He grumbled on the ground, in the plane, and going down; and nothing, not even a landing on the exact center of the target, made him smile.

"Corporal, you are being asked to do the most difficult jumping I have ever seen in all my years in the military," Sergeant Fuqua reassured him.

"Fuck you," Contardo always responded, a response which, given the special circumstances, Sergeant Fuqua chose to reinterpret as something other than insubordination.

Like a doctor dealing with a very ill, very difficult patient, Sergeant Fuqua noted that Contardo showed "great progress" and "was coming along nicely."

"Fuck you again," Contardo would say, and

again Sergeant Fuqua would smile.

One near mishap almost cost the Rangers O'Connor. After a month on Lonelyville, during a night run, the Catalina had to make a pass over the island from the ocean. The exercise required the Rangers to jump virtually at once and land all together on the same spot. Only the most accomplished airborne acrobats attempt such derring-do.

"This kind of paratrooping, men, is not only difficult, but also dangerous," Sergeant Fuqua warned before their first attempt. "If I had not been told you have to learn this, I would forbid you from ever doing it."

The Rangers had been practicing. They would jump at twice the normal altitude—1500 feet.

As well as anyone could tell later, O'Connor anticipated the count and simply jumped too soon. That happens all the time and isn't necessarily dangerous. But, when O'Connor jumped, an unusually hearty gust of wind came up off the Pacific knocking the big Irishman back against the Catalina and causing the chute lines to catch on the tail. Within seconds O'Connor found himself dangling upside down, flapping in the night sky.

At that moment Corrigan got serious and forgot his longstanding feud with the Rangers.

"I can feel him on the tail," he said matter-of-factly. "I can feel the drag. Hold my baby here steady and I'll go out and get him."

"Thanks, but that's my job. I'm the Lone Ranger. Remember? Just keep her up and even." McLeane's voice lacked enthusiasm. Under such circumstances his voice usually lacked enthusiasm.

"Ever done this before?" Corrigan asked.

"I've been out on the wing a couple of times."

"At night?"

McLeane let that one pass.

"I can see him, sir," said Wilkins hanging out the door of the plane.

"That's good," said McLeane to himself, "because we can't put a light out there."

Without a word the Rangers had already begun to work. Finding long pieces of guideline from earlier practices, they spliced them together and tied them first around McLeane and then around each other. They fastened the end to an exposed, metal support rod.

McLeane ran his hands over his face and shook his head. Maybe someday he would live a normal life.

He backed out of the plane holding on to the top of the hatch. The wind had suddenly become fierce. He looked over his right shoulder and could see a dark shadow swaying below the tail of the plane. He looked up and saw two hooks above the hatch. He had no idea what they might be for otherwise, but he used them to swing himself on top of the Catalina. He gave the guideline a couple of loops around one of the hooks. Fortunately, the Catalina, as with a lot of sea planes, had been built like a box. He could move with some ease to the tail. Once there, he had to get out to O'Connor.

For a moment, McLeane considered going back and having Corrigan drop the Catalina in the water. But the impact, no matter how gentle, would probably knock him out and he could drown by the time anyone cut him loose. He couldn't set him loose in the air. Cut the lines and O'Connor had no chute. McLeane had to get at least part of O'Connor on the Catalina. And he might not have much time. As far as anyone knew, O'Connor could have strangled to death out there.

McLeane eased himself out onto the narrowing rear of the fuselage. He slid along slowly to the tail. The wind made his eyes tear. He could not see O'Connor at all. Like a snake he bellied to the end of the Catalina and then slithered onto the tail. He found a place to hook his left foot. With visibility zero and only one hand free, he felt beneath him. He could grab parachute lines. He had no idea how O'Connor might be tangled. What would happen if he just pulled them?

"O'Connor? You O.K.?"

What a dumb question, McLeane thought to himself. With the wind and the engines who could hear him anyway? He should save his breath. He had a hard enough time just breathing. But something made him want to call out.

"You down there, O'Connor?"

Intelligent question number two.

Suddenly, using his free hand, he grabbed and tugged. Nothing moved. Lines were caught everywhere, but the chute seemed untorn. McLeane just kept pulling, shaking the lines.

Then he took another chance. Letting go with his anchored foot, he moved still farther out on the tail. He could feel a tangle of parachute lines and part of the chute.

What a mess, he thought to himself.

37

In his mind he wanted to pull O'Connor up onto the plane. But the idea, at that moment, seemed ridiculous. Frustrated, he just tore at the jumble in front of him. In an instant the chute came loose.

"Aaaahhh!"

McLeane sensed a body falling.

Without a thought he cut his guideline free. He prayed Corrigan had kept them over the ocean. He dropped from the tail of the plane. Below him he could see what looked like a chute. Was it opened or closed? He couldn't tell. He let himself drop as much as he dared, then pulled the cord. He saw the shine off the water, heard a splash. He had a pretty good idea where O'Connor hit. Just yards from landing, McLeane slipped out of his parachute, entered the water with his arms out at his sides, and began swimming.

Suddenly he heard another sound.

"Is that you, O'Connor?"

A reply came at once.

"Who the fuck do you think it is?"

"I thought it was you."

The two men swam toward each other.

"May I see your pass for night swimming, O'Connor."

"You know, Major, you ask some pretty stupid questions."

"I'm practicing to be a newspaper reporter."

"Jesus, 'O'Connor? You O.K.?' How the fuck can I be O.K.? I'm hanging upside down 1500 feet in the fucking air by my fucking leg, and you want to know if I'm O.K."

They could hear and then see the Catalina landing.

"Well, you look O.K.," said McLeane.

The Rangers dragged both of them into the plane.

"Then he wants to know if I'm down there," O'Connor continued without dropping a syllable. "First he wants to know if I'm O.K. Then he wants to know if it's me. Then when he sees me in the water, it's a big surprise. 'Is that you, O'Connor?' 'No, it's not me. Why should it be me? It's Rita Hayworth.' For a smart man, sir, you can ask some pretty stupid questions."

McLeane shrugged, laughing, relieved.

"Next time I'll work on asking better questions."

"What happened up there?" Corrigan called back from the cockpit.

"O'Connor will tell you when we hit camp."

The Catalina taxied back to the island where Sergeant Fuqua insisted on a full account of "the celestial goings on" as Contardo called them.

At once, Sergeant Fuqua canceled exercises for two days, but the Rangers complained.

"It was a freak accident," said O'Connor. "Could happen anytime, anywhere, and never happen again."

"I'm for going right back up tonight," said Contardo.

"Me too," Heinman and Wilkins chimed in together.

McLeane smiled, with more than a little pride. Nothing short of death would stop these guys, and he wasn't sure of death.

"They're some bunch," Corrigan said as everyone broke for camp.

Sergeant Fuqua decided to resume exercises tomorrow, wind permitting.

"Yeah, they're a tough group of guys."

Before going to sleep, O'Connor walked over to where McLeane lay thinking and chain-smoking Chesterfields.

"Thanks for saving my life, Mack," he said.

"You're welcome," said McLeane without looking at him.

Nothing more needed to be said. McLeane liked it when his men called him Mack.

During their stay in Lonelyville, the Rangers learned to jump as well as anyone in any branch of the service at any time. So, at least, said Sergeant Fuqua, who ought to know, and Sergeant Barlow agreed. That part of the mission accomplished, General Thompson sent word, through Corrigan, that the Rangers were to return to Vella La Vella.

Before leaving the island, they said goodbye to the two men from the 101st who had taught them an awful lot of what they knew. Goodbye came as a silent handshake. Contardo added, "Thanks." O'Connor just stood there and shook his head for a while.

"No more night swimming, O'Connor," said Sergeant Fuqua.

"Not bad for an Army man, Sarge."

"I'll take that as a compliment."

McLeane said something appropriate. Everyone waved. Corrigan fired up the engines. The Catalina headed back to someplace closer to civilization.

Four

After almost two months in the air over Lonely-ville, the sandy ground of Vella La Vella felt good to Ranger feet. Margot, calmer than when they parted, greeted McLeane with a warm hug and a kiss.

"I love you, Mack," she said loud enough for everyone to hear as they all departed the Catalina.

McLeane shook his head and held her tight.

The other Rangers headed straight for their tents.

General Archie Thompson waited for McLeane to shower and shave. He even let him eat dinner, sleep, and have breakfast the next morning. Only then did he decide on a briefing.

"Mack, it's time to talk," Thompson said as McLeane finished his second cup of coffee.

"I know," Thompson added defensively, "I keep barging in while you want to be alone with

Margot. I know you haven't been back a day yet. I know you deserve a rest.''

He stood over the breakfast table with his hat in his hand.

''I know. I know. I know,'' he went on until Margot got up.

''Please sit down, General,'' she said graciously. ''I have more coffee.''

McLeane had become used to General Thompson sitting at his table, standing at his door, outside his window. He even rather liked old Archie, with his gray crew cut, constant frown, and nervous stomach, and normally he would have been more than hospitable.

On that particular morning, however, Maj. H. D. Flagg had accompanied General Thompson to the quarters of Major McLeane. McLeane had less use for Flagg than for any Jap fighting in the Pacific. Along with being a wimp and a bureaucrat, Flagg also managed to be wrong—all of the time. At that moment he stood by the entrance to the room where McLeane and Margot had been eating breakfast.

Thompson, aware of the deep disaffection the two men held for each other, hoped, nevertheless, that McLeane might still abide by the ancient laws of hospitality and invite Flagg to the table anyway.

McLeane just nodded and Thompson, relieved, beckoned Flagg.

''Try to be civil, Mack,'' the general whispered.

''Major McLeane,'' Flagg said, extending a hand.

''Major Flagg.''

They shook hands.

McLeane noted the glasses, the sincere, but pompous look, the too-firm handshake, the clipboard.

"Don't ask too much, sir," he whispered to General Thompson.

The two men sat down.

Margot brought a fresh pot of coffee and cups.

"Real coffee," Flagg remarked as Margot poured.

"See what I mean?" McLeane said to Thompson.

"O.K. Let's get down to cases here," Thompson said, ignoring McLeane's comment. "Mack, you're going to New Guinea."

McLeane had the distinct impression that New Guinea should mean something special to him.

"O.K," he said simply.

"Don't you know who's there?" Flagg asked.

"MacArthur," replied McLeane with a shrug.

Thompson interrupted.

"My friend General Bramley needs help. He can't seem to take or bypass Hill 457. He's got an entire division tied up, and he's losing men right and left.

"That hill commands a pass through the Stanley's, the mountains which run through the length of the island. In other words that hill has got to go."

"The Rangers have to take 457," McLeane paraphrased.

"The Rangers have to take 457," Thompson nodded.

"Yes, the Rangers have to take 457," Flagg added.

"One more thing," Thompson went on, "four-fifty-seven is fortified in typical Japanese fashion. They have a labyrinth of tunnels and a million entrances from which to attack our men. Our artillery can't touch them, and the infantry assaults are pure suicide.''

"How about the Air Force?" McLeane volunteered.

"Won't work.''

"May I ask why, sir?"

"Major Flagg will take over." General Thompson gestured to his left.

Major Flagg readied his clipboard, shuffled papers on the table, removed a pen from his pocket.

"We, that is Marine Corps Intelligence," Flagg began, "have concluded that the only way to take 457 is by a commando attack. This attack will come as a parachute drop right on the top of the hill.

"Now the hill is poorly defended at the top. The Japs must think that nobody will get that far. We, that is Marine Corps Intelligence knows . . . we know the Japs have only a few sentries in a machine-gun trench up there. They get to the top and down again via a vertical shaft that connects to a network of other tunnels."

Flagg started to sketch a diagram. McLeane stopped him.

"That's all right. I got the picture," he said. "And the Japs use the bottom of the vertical shaft to store munitions."

"Yes," said Flagg nonplused. "How did you know?"

"Everyone knows, Major. Every swinging Richard in any kind of uniform on this island knows.

44

Even my mother knows.''

''Well, the Japanese must think that a safe place for their ammunition, and maybe it is because we have determined that a bombardier would have a million-to-one shot at hitting the opening.''

Here Flagg got excited.

''Think about it, Mack.'' He corrected himself quickly. ''Think about it, Major. A bombardier has to hit a five-foot-wide shaft from an altitude of no lower than seven hundred fifty feet. Probably, he'd have to fly higher and probably he'd have to go at night because he hasn't a snowball's chance in hell during the day.''

Flagg's eyes lit up.

''But a surprise visit by a Ranger group and a special, spherical land mine built by O'Connor could do the trick.''

Flagg looked at McLeane who looked at Thompson.

''Let me see if I understand this, sir,'' he said to the general. The Rangers are supposed to parachute on to four-fifty-seven, knock out a few defenders, and roll a magic ball made by O'Connor down a vertical shaft which connects to lots of tunnels. The magic ball explodes. We win the war, and everyone goes home a hero.''

General Thompson said nothing.

''Of course, there's more to it, Major McLeane.''

McLeane's voice had taken on a slight edge.

''Flagg, I hope there's a lot more to it.''

''We, that is Marine—''

''Cut it.''

''The bomb is based on something similar used

45

by the RAF against the Germans in the Ruhr. It's about three feet wide, weighs one hundred pounds and—''

''Someone has to carry it going down.''

''Yes.''

At that point, McLeane got to his feet and began pacing the room.

''With all due respect, sir,'' he said, addressing General Thompson, ''have you reviewed these plans?''

''I have, Mack.''

''And you think this makes sense?''

General Thompson hesitated.

''I know it sounds awfully . . .'' He struggled until he came up with the word *complicated*.

He paused.

''Maybe complicated isn't the word,'' he added.

McLeane stopped pacing.

''Margot,'' he called. ''Margot!''

Red Bird came on the double.

''Mack, is something wrong?''

''What do we have to drink around here?''

''I don't know.''

''Find something, Margot, anything.''

McLeane flopped back in his chair and slumped down.

''Someone in this room is a raving lunatic. Maybe it's me.''

Flagg ventured to speak.

''If it will put your mind at ease—''

''Oh, please, Flagg—put my mind at ease. You're such a reassuring guy.''

Margot came with a bottle of something. Mc-

Leane didn't look to see what it was, but poured it into his cup on top of the coffee and took a giant swallow. He passed the bottle to Thompson.

"Sorry, Flagg, but this reassures me," he said holding up the fortified coffee. "Continue."

"Marine Corps Intelligence also has determined that you will have an easy time getting away down the north side of the mountain.

"You see, once you drop the bomb down the shaft, you radio MacArthur's troops or Bramley's troops on the island and they attack from the south side. This will draw all the Japanese away from your escape."

"Did the same guys who dreamed up this plan come up with this information?"

"This has all been carefully worked out by Marine Corps Intelligence."

McLeane turned to Thompson.

"What are my options, sir?"

"Well, Mack, you can always refuse," said General Thompson in such a way that McLeane knew he could not refuse.

He sat in silence for a long moment; then he looked at both men.

"You must know how utterly preposterous this whole plan is."

"Marine Corps Intelligence has done its homework well," said Flagg proudly.

"That does not reassure me, Flagg."

McLeane poured another shot.

"What is that, Major?" Flagg asked.

McLeane gave the man a withering glance.

"If there's nothing more to be done here, sir"—

Flagg turned to Thompson—"I'd like to be excused."

"You're excused," said Thompson, his thoughts someplace else.

The two majors shook hands perfunctorily, and Flagg left.

Margot poked her head into the tent, saw General Thompson still sitting with McLeane, and disappeared again.

No one said anything for a long time.

"Aren't there a lot of Australian forces on New Guinea?" McLeane asked General Thompson.

"Two logistics divisions, and, of course, my old friend Bramley is an Aussie."

"He heads the Allied Land Forces doesn't he?"

"Yes and a damn good man."

General Thompson finished his cup of fortified morning coffee.

"Well, maybe Corrigan will have someone to talk to."

Thompson poured himself a fast shot and downed it quickly.

"I'm glad you'll do it, Mack."

McLeane just nodded.

"I'm proud of you," said General Thompson getting up to go. "We're all proud of you."

McLeane sat, staring at the table, his cup held with both hands and nodded. He was lost in thought.

General Thompson let himself out.

Major Imamura stood alone, protected by the bamboo hideout General Sasaki called headquarters, and watched the rain, unusual for October, pound the jungle. The water had already made deep ponds and rivers in places where none existed before. A flood out of season would alter the war for both sides. Imamura smiled at the thought of American and Japanese generals throwing away their best-laid strategies and coming up with new ones especially for wet weather.

He heard hard footsteps behind him and felt the general's stern presence at his back. In silence they watched the rain together.

"You have studied these Rangers how long?" General Sasaki asked finally.

"One week," replied Imamura.

"You can destroy them for the Emperor?"

"I can destroy them for the Emperor."

The general did not like the young major's casual answers and the relaxed way in which he behaved with superiors present. But Major Imamura came highly recommended, so General Sasaki would tolerate him.

"What will you need?" asked the general.

Imamura hesitated only slightly.

"I will give you eight men and no more," the general snapped at once and left, thinking on his way out that the time Imamura had spent in America had addled his brain.

For his part Imamura did not turn to see the general go.

Always be suspicious of any man who wears a sword in the rain, he thought to himself.

At least he had the promise of eight men, more than he had a week ago, and some vague idea of what to do. Exactly how he would make McLeane's Rangers disappear so Sasaki could sleep at night remained another problem. For all the information Intelligence had given him, they forgot to mention where the Rangers might be as he sat and watched the rain fall.

With Sasaki gone, he felt free to sit down and have a Chesterfield, which he did.

McLeane collected his thoughts; then he decided to brief the Rangers at once on their new mission. Luckily, he found them all together, across the clearing, in the part of the camp they called home. They had just finished straightening their quarters, putting things away, and getting themselves back to normal after having been gone for almost two months.

As McLeane approached, they knew something had to be not quite right. Heinman called them all outside.

"Why do you think the Old Man's coming?" Contardo asked.

"He wants to discuss the results of the World Series."

"What would we do without you O'Connor?"

"Well, I think," said Wilkins slowly, "he's got a job for us to do."

"Keep thinking like that, Wilkins," said Contardo, "and they'll make you a general."

"Listen up, men," McLeane said before he'd even stopped walking. "We've got a job."

They all went into the radio shack and McLeane, as quickly as possible, told them as much as he knew. Then he stood silent.

"Any questions?"

"Yes, sir," said Contardo. "Would you repeat everything after 'Listen up, men.' "

Everyone laughed, as much from nerves as anything else.

"They want us to jump onto a hill with a hundred-pound bomb that I'm supposed to make, kill a handful of Japs, throw the bomb down a hole, and leave, right?" asked O'Connor.

"Something like that," said McLeane.

"They're nuts. They are all fucking nuts," said Contardo, the self-appointed philosopher of the group.

While everyone else sat around in disbelief, Wilkins wore a big smile on his face.

"May I ask why you're smiling, Wilkins?"

"You may, sir."

"O.K. Wilkins, why are you smiling?"

"Because we are going to get to kick some more Japanese ass."

They all stopped talking for a minute.

"Well, when you put it that way," said Contardo, "it changes everything."

"When do we leave, sir?" Heinman asked.

"How long will it take you to make the bomb, O'Connor?"

"One like that RAF job? Jesus, I don't know. How the hell do I know? I got no plans, no materials. You officers are something, sir. I have got to say that."

"How long, O'Connor?"

O'Connor thought for a while.

"Give me everything I want and I can do it in . . ."

He paused to check his calculations.

"Four or five days. I can't do better than that."

"Good," said McLeane. "You've got forty-eight hours, and if I know anything about supplies around here, you'll only get about half the things you need."

"Think of the challenge," Wilkins offered.

"You're carrying the fucking thing down," said O'Connor. "And while I make the fucking thing you can hold the dynamite."

"Listen, men, I know how you feel," said McLeane seriously. "I really do. I feel the same way. But we've always done the job. We can be proud of that."

The Rangers walked outside with him. He started across the clearing, turned, and gave them the thumbs up sign.

"Thanks," they heard him say.

"What do you do with a guy like that?" Contardo asked Heinman.

"Whatever he tells you."

Within an hour O'Connor had the plan for the bomb and a requisition signed by General Thompson for half of everything he needed to make it.

Five

After less than a week Maj. Jinichi Imamura had collected eight experienced and iron-willed Japanese soldiers for his cadre of Commandos. Imamura had worked personally with the three from the Special Naval Landing Force.

Yasu Nara, captain, age 23, earned his wings as a fighter pilot and could parachute from any height onto a dime.

Akira Nagasaki, sergeant, age 27, competed unsuccessfully for Japan in the 1936 Olympics. Even as a loser, however, he could still outrun anyone in both armies. He also knew weapons.

Toshitane Takata, lieutenant, age 29, attended the University of Pennsylvania where he majored in American history. Outside of a general toughness and a knowledge of the English language and American customs no greater, actually, than Imamura's,

Takata had no real reason to be among the commandos except that Imamura liked him; they could speak English together and share common experiences. Moreover, as graduates of Ivy League universities, each, in his own way, had an intense dislike for Columbia, McLeane's alma mater.

The other five commandos came to Imamura by recommendation.

Hideki Tojo, sergeant, age 22, excelled as an all-around athlete and marksman.

Korechika Anami, corporal, age 22, graduated top in his class at Tokyo's Royal Military Institute for Special Training. He had proven himself several times already in the war as a crack underwater demolition expert.

Honsu Atsugi, sergeant, age 31, taught martial arts to Japanese Marine officers at the Tokyo Institute.

Sanji Iwabuchi, captain, age 30, graduated as an electrical engineer from the University of Kyoto and subsequently became expert in making and using explosives.

Takeo Kurito, private, age 21, grew up in the South Pacific, knew the people, the geography, and many of the dialects.

Major Imamura liked the men he had gathered around him not only because each displayed a particular skill, demonstrated courage, and could be called upon as a reliable soldier, but also because none of them had the slightest desire to die for the Emperor.

After his many years in America, Imamura found the Japanese need to commit suicide in time of war disturbing. In time of war Imamura had always thought killing the other guy should be the object. He always had a great need to come out alive, have a good meal, a few drinks, and enjoy the company of a woman or two. To do those things he had fought the war. From what he could tell his men felt the same way.

General Sasaki had quartered the commandos in a small jungle clearing near his own mountain head-quarters. There the nine lived primitively, in tents. During the day, they exercised. But since the men had little experience as a group, Imamura planned short missions for them. They retrieved each other from swamps and crocodile-infested waters, and helped each other across ravines at night.

Good to begin with, in no time the commandos got better. After a couple of weeks, Major Imamura could look at his men with assurance. In any skir-mish they would do the job.

After a couple of weeks, too, General Sasaki made a surprise visit one day at noon mess. All the commandos bowed when he entered the group and stood for forty-five minutes while he praised Hiro-hito and abused MacArthur, Roosevelt, Churchill, and Stalin before he left. The men returned to their fish and rice.

"Is he always like that, Major?" Lieutenant Takata asked Imamura.

"Like what?"

"Like he's angry all the time."

"Yes, he's always like that."

Takata went on eating.

"And he always wears his sword," Imamura

added. "Even when it rains."

The next few days wore on Imamura and his commandos. Without orders to fight they had nothing to do but wait.

Since he'd returned from briefing the Rangers, Margot had watched McLeane, watched him pour and drink a cup of cold coffee; pick up, read, and put down a battered copy of Hemingway's *To Have and Have Not;* go to the window, sit down at the table, and figure something with pencil and paper; go inside and lie down; come out, do more figuring; drink more cold coffee and go to the window again.

"Mack?" Margot asked half afraid to say anything at all. "Did everything go all right with the men?"

"Yes," he said, not really paying attention.

"Did they take it well?"

He looked over at her.

"Better than they should have." His voice took on an edge of anger. "A hell of a lot better than they should have."

Margot decided to say nothing, there being little she could say.

They stood silently together.

"I'll tell you this, Margot," McLeane exploded. "if that four-eyed squirrel, Flagg, isn't one hundred percent right and if I come back in one piece, I will cripple him with these."

He showed her his hands like a surgeon scrubbing down. She took them in her own and kissed them.

"I'll kill him."

Margot felt the rage in his body, but said nothing.

"Nobody knows how good my guys are, Margot. Nobody knows what they do out there, how many times they save themselves from dying only to save themselves again, themselves, me, each other, and these . . . these . . ."

Language failed him.

"They're crazy. All of them from Roosevelt on down. Thompson is 'proud,' and Flagg is 'positive,' and they sit back here and eat New Zealand lamb and drink real coffee and make plans."

"This one's bad, isn't it, Mack?" Margot dared to say.

"Bad?" McLeane pulled away from her. "Bad? This plan is outrageous. It's suicide."

McLeane stopped himself. He never discussed this part of his job with Margot or with anyone else for that matter.

"If *they* had to do any of what they want *us* to do, there wouldn't be a mission. That's a guarantee."

Margot had never heard McLeane talk like this before. She put her arms around him. McLeane did not fear for himself. That much Margot knew. He had no real fear of death. But he had become fiercely protective of his men. He did not like the way the higher command used them, put them on the line again and again. Margot also knew he could do nothing about it. Major William McLeane would be a soldier first last and always. She'd just heard an outburst of frustration.

"Come with me," she said. McLeane let himself be led to the bed.

"I've got something for you," she said with a

57

wicked smile.

Margot slowly unbuttoned her blouse. She unhooked her bra and just as slowly removed it.

She was beautiful, McLeane thought to himself, almost worth the war.

Her white breasts shimmering, she moved toward him and dropped to her knees.

"Lie back," she said and pushed him gently.

She unzipped his fly. Every part of his body sprang to attention.

"You're going to have to relax more, Major," she said working him up and down, kissing him, washing him with her tongue.

"We're going to have to put him at ease," Margot continued impishly and nibbled at the top of his cock.

She giggled as he squirmed and let out a "Jesus."

Her mouth went to work, and McLeane felt a rush of pleasure. He reached down and tied his fingers in her hair, her hair, her beautiful, red hair, her beautiful, long, red hair. When he could stand it no longer, he leaned forward and pulled Margot to her feet.

"Take that off," he said hoarsely, pointing at her clothes.

"Suppose I don't want to," she said playfully.

"O.K. I'll do it," said McLeane, throbbing all over. "If that's the way you want it."

In a flash he had her around the knees and had thrown her on the bed. As they both laughed, he wrestled her stark naked.

"You're awful," she said with nothing between

herself and McLeane's fierce passion.

"You started this, and I'm going to finish it." He moved between her legs.

Margot gave a quick start as he entered her.

"Oh, Mack," she said, half out of breath.

"Major to you."

She just gasped.

Suddenly, McLeane thrust himself all the way into her.

"I love you," she said.

They made love all afternoon and late into the evening. Sometime before midnight, McLeane lit a Chesterfield. Margot just lay next to him with her eyes closed. Neither spoke for a while.

McLeane broke the silence. "I'm hungry."

Margot opened her eyes. "There's nothing to eat."

"There must be something open all night around here," said McLeane. "Shall we drop in on the Japanese mess? Why don't we call ahead to the Jap Sixth Army, order two from A and one from B."

"That's Chinese."

"Chinese, Japanese, what's the difference?"

"We're fighting the Japanese, not the Chinese. But let me at least get you a drink."

She got out of bed and McLeane watched the cheeks of her ass bounce, his passion stirring a bit.

She handed him a cup of the same vile alcohol he had shared with Thompson that morning.

"What do you think you'll do after the war, Mack?" Margot said casually as she climbed into bed.

"Haven't given it any thought," McLeane said

as the fiery liquid went down his throat like splinters.

"Do you think you'll go back to school?"

"Maybe."

"Do you think you'll settle down?"

"Maybe."

McLeane could not imagine what it would be like after the war. For him the future only meant another mission.

"Do you think . . . ?"

"I don't think anything," McLeane responded, turning out the battery-run torch used for a night light and rolling over. In the dark he reached over to touch her.

"Do you love me?" she asked.

"Yes."

He felt Margot snuggle closer to him.

McLeane woke to the sound of someone yelling outside the tent. He pulled on his pants and headed for the sound of the noise. There before him stood Contardo and Heinman.

"Let me guess," he said, his mouth raw, his eyes half-closed. "Contardo was doing all the yelling, right?"

"On the money again, sir," said Contardo with a broad smile.

"We didn't mean to bother you," Heinman said. "But we thought you would want to know that O'Connor has finished making the bomb."

McLeane could only chuckle.

"What happened to the four or five days he absolutely needed?"

"Well, Wilkins helped him."

"So did I," said Contardo. "And so did Adolf here."

"We all did," Heinman said.

"I held the light," Contardo added proudly.

"You were up all night?" McLeane wanted to know.

"Damn near," said Contardo.

Clearly, these two men felt good about what they had just done.

"Where's O'Connor now?"

"He and Wilkins are both sacked out," Heinman answered.

"Mack! Mack!"

Suddenly Margot came running out of the tent, wrapping a robe around herself. She stopped short when she saw Heinman and Contardo.

"Oh, I'm sorry."

McLeane went over and put his arm around her. Contardo and Heinman looked embarrassed.

"What's up, beautiful," McLeane said casually.

"I woke up and you weren't there and I heard voices and . . . I don't know."

Margot buried her head in McLeane's shoulder. McLeane kissed her on the head.

"Go back to bed," he said gently.

"Sorry, fellas," Margot said to Contardo and Heinman.

"Hey, that's O.K.," said Contardo.

"She's nervous," said McLeane when Margot was gone. "You two get some rest."

The men nodded and disappeared.

McLeane looked at his watch. He had slept until

almost noon. He would have to tell Thompson and that idiot Flagg that O'Connor had finished the bomb.

McLeane met Thompson and Flagg at a small canteen erected on Vella La Vella for the benefit of all troops. McLeane said only that the Rangers were ready.

General Thompson nodded his gray crew-cut head. Flagg got all excited.

"We're ready to move out," he said, like a child going to an amusement park.

McLeane ignored the misuse of "we're." Even if Flagg insisted, McLeane wouldn't take him along on a mission.

"How quickly can you move out?" Thompson asked.

"Forty-eight hours." McLeane stirred his coffee.

"It would be better, sir, if they could move out sooner," Flagg said to General Thompson.

Thompson looked at McLeane.

"Why, Major?" Thompson asked Flagg.

"Those troops have been pounding that hill a long time, sir."

McLeane let that one pass, too.

"What will another few hours matter, Flagg?" Thompson asked.

"Intelligence reports show that the Japanese are particularly vulnerable at this moment."

McLeane did not let that one go by.

"What do you mean 'intelligence reports show that the Japanese are particularly vulnerable at this time'?'' McLeane tried to control himself. "The Rangers are particularly vulnerable at this time. O'Connor and Wilkins just went to sleep after being up all night."

"MacArthur's troops need . . ."

"Forty-eight hours."

That's all McLeane said before he walked out of the canteen.

Twenty minutes later a messenger carried a note of apology to McLeane from General Thompson.

"Sorry," it read. "Forty-eight hours it is. Good Luck."

McLeane rumpled the note and threw it across the room, angry that he hadn't asked for forty-eight days.

Six

Military air transports invariably were either too hot or too cold, but the Catalina managed to achieve both extremes. The Rangers huddled together for warmth or complained of the heat.

McLeane sat next to Corrigan in the copilot's seat and looked out into the black.

"Here I am in the fucking Pacific, three thousand degrees hot and freezing my ass off at the same time," he heard Contardo yell above the noise of the engines. "It's a weird fucking war."

Corrigan hadn't said much since the flight started. When they all boarded, he just looked at McLeane and swore once again that if anything happened to the Catalina, he would make sure none of the Rangers came back.

"Why don't you and the Catalina get married," McLeane suggested.

"We are."

Since then McLeane had not heard much from Corrigan.

"You O.K.?" he asked the dour Aussie.

"Fine, just fucking fine."

He turned and looked at McLeane.

"This is the craziest one yet, McLeane."

"Don't blame me. It isn't my idea."

McLeane had a flashlight and a navigator's map in front of him.

"I've got to find one fucking hill, a pinpoint in the dark, hit it so that five guys can jump onto it at the same time and not get shot down."

"You can do it," McLeane said, trying to loosen Corrigan a little.

"Of course I can do it," Corrigan replied. "But I'm sick of doing it all the fucking time. This plane's been through enough," he said.

Corrigan couldn't be too upset, McLeane thought. He's back to his same, old arrogant self.

"Give me a reading, McLeane, if it's not too much trouble."

McLeane checked the instrument panel, then the map, then the instrument panel again.

"You're doing fine. We're at about two-seven-four degrees magnetic. Almost due west, a couple of degrees north. Right on target. How much longer have we got to go?"

"We just took off, for Christ's sake. A couple hours if we don't run into any unexpected wind."

The Rangers were quiet.

"Check your equipment," McLeane yelled back at them.

"We checked it a thousand fucking times already," Contardo yelled back.

"Check your chutes."

"We checked them already," Contardo said.

"Check them again."

They checked their chutes again.

"Have you got your orders, Corrigan?"

"What are you the mother hen? Of course, I've got my orders. After I drop you gents off, I go fishing."

The thought brought a broad grin to Corrigan's face.

"Yes, sir. After I drop you gents off, I lay up on Masini with my old pole—if you get my drift—and fish, fish for bonita, fish for native girls with comfortable titties. You shall be always in my thoughts, McLeane."

"Okay, but don't forget to pick us up."

"Nothing would make me happier. I shall be waiting for your call."

If Corrigan and the Rangers did not always get along, the Aussie could always be relied upon to do the job. McLeane knew that. So did the Rangers.

In the back of the plane, O'Connor made sure that Wilkins had the bomb properly secured. It looked like a giant bowling ball nestled like a baby in a papoose strapped to Wilkins' chest.

"You realize, Wilkins," O'Connor said seriously, "that if anything happens to you on the drop, this whole mission don't mean shit."

"Of course I realize that."

"So my dumb, cracker friend," O'Connor went on, "you had best do everything right, or I shall find your Georgia ass and kick it all the way back to the Statue of Liberty. Do you read me?''

"Nothing bad ever happens to me, and nothing ever will.'' So said Wilkins, a broad grin on his face.

Contardo wanted action, but the jump had him a little nervous. The war don't start 'til I get there, Contardo thought to himself. And I don't get there 'til my feet touch the ground.

Heinman had stopped figuring the odds of making the mission work. They had been in trouble before and would probably be in trouble again. Just do the job and don't think about anything else. That had always been his dictum, and it had worked for him so far. He sat there letting his mind go blank.

"Give me another reading,'' Corrigan snapped.

"We're getting there. Same reading as before.''

"We have less than an hour. I'll be calling for readings a lot now.''

"You get 'em.''

Except for the readings, no one spoke.

Soon, they all realized how close the time had come when each one of them would put himself on the line one more time. The plane tensed.

"Give me an absolutely accurate reading, Mack.''

"I have an absolute two-seven-four. North of west.''

"O.K. I'm taking her up. Give me a reading when we should be approaching the coast. I'll cut the engines, and we'll glide in.''

The Catalina turned upward and started gaining altitude rapidly. Then, just as rapidly, the Catalina leveled off.

"Have you thought, Wilkins, old buddy," said O'Connor, "that if you get shot in the bomb as we go down, nobody will ever find your pieces."

"Nothing ever happens to me, and nothing ever will," was the reply one more time.

"Cocky little bastard," muttered O'Connor.

Contardo had turned several shades of green thinking of the jump.

Heinman had himself under control. His nerves were steel.

"O.K." said McLeane, "We should be over the coast in about seven minutes and thirty-three seconds. If we could see anything, we would be able to see the coast by now."

"I'm cutting the engine," Corrigan announced. "From here on we glide down."

"We're lucky. There's no wind."

"This is still ridiculous."

With no engine noise the plane became ominously silent. Everyone could feel the plane dropping.

"Can you see anything, hero?"

"Not really, but I should be able to make out something soon."

"Either they haven't spotted us, or they're waiting for us to get closer before opening up."

The Catalina continued to make its quiet descent undisturbed.

"Why do I hang around you Yanks, anyway?" Corrigan muttered to himself.

"Pure love," McLeane told him.

"Love, my—"

"Don't break my heart, Corrigan. I see the coast

69

line. We should be passing over it in seconds.''

"You'd better get back there and get ready. I'll find this fucking hill on my own.''

"Thanks, Corrigan.''

"Go fuck yourself.''

"You're such a sweetheart. When the war is over, will you marry *me?*''

"Get the fuck out of here. I'm already married . . . to my baby here.''

Corrigan patted the instrument panel. It was a habit of his, but he had done it more often on this mission, McLeane noted.

The Rangers saw McLeane emerging from the cockpit.

"Get in place,'' he said very quietly. "Corrigan will give the signal. I'll be a split second behind; otherwise we're doing this together.''

The Rangers stood in a line before the door. McLeane checked his watch, went to say something to Corrigan, and then returned and opened the door.

McLeane could see not one light below, only vague shadows. This would be like jumping off the end of the world.

Suddenly, they saw Corrigan's small flashlight.

"Go,'' McLeane said. He touched all four of them at the same time and then dropped himself. Contardo's chute opened first, then O'Connor's, Wilkins', then Heinman's.

Contardo kept his eyes closed all the way down. Look around, Heinman had told him. Enjoy the view. Fuck Heinman, Contardo thought. He did not want to know. With his eyes shut tight he could smell his mother's marinara sauce wafting over

70

Flatbush Avenue. Would he ever eat another bowl of pasta again? Would he ever see Pee Wee Reese making a backhanded save again? Would the Dodgers win another Series? Would he ever live to see them do it? His hands perspired on the chute lines. He looked down. He couldn't see a damned thing. He had a great need at the moment to just piss all over the world.

Suddenly, McLeane lost sight of Wilkins. Contardo, Heinman, and O'Connor all drifted down just feet below him and not far from one another. But he could not see Wilkins. His eyes scanned the sky in vain.

As the Rangers neared the hill, they had their weapons ready. They anticipated getting hung up on a tall banyan tree. That didn't happen. Although they did not land exactly where they should have, they hit not far away.

McLeane heard flak, first 20-mm fire. Were they firing from jeeps or emplacements? McLeane asked himself. Then he heard the 155s open up. The Japanese had found Corrigan. The Catalina's engines roared to life. Silently, McLeane wished Corrigan luck. Just before touching down, he checked his .45 and the 6.5-mm carbine. Both had been fitted with silencers. He still could not see Wilkins. Had the Japs seen them? That's what he wanted to know.

Heinman and O'Connor came down easily. Contardo's parachute seemed to have the usual snags. He wrestled with it until Heinman went over and cut him free.

For a moment the four men just stood there. So far they had been extremely fortunate. All of them knew that. According to intelligence, only a few sentries and lookouts in a machine-gun trench guarded the top of the hill. They'd landed not far from the hilltop. But they had to find Wilkins.

Without a word, as though all were parts of one large body, the Rangers fanned out. Even if they had to keep silence, they would manage to stay in contact.

Normally, McLeane did without a compass. But the drop threw him off. He checked his bearings on a small compass with a green fluorescent dial. He had last seen Wilkins drifting south-southwest, maybe a hundred yards from the pack. O'Connor had already moved in that direction. The other Rangers followed.

Moving quietly through areca palm and nano shrub and maomori leaves was hard enough in day light. At night it proved impossible. The Rangers sounded to McLeane like a herd of elephants going through the jungle brush. In the dark with dead eyes, the other senses come alive, and he felt sure the Japanese could hear them coming.

Suddenly, everyone stopped. They found themselves at the same clearing. Twenty feet from where they stood, clearly visible against the shadow of the nano shrub, loomed a white parachute. On the ground hidden by leaves and vines, lay Wilkins, quite alive but unable to move.

No one spoke a word. McLeane felt the bones in Wilkins' body. By the way Wilkins moved when McLeane touched his left ankle, they could both tell something had to be wrong.

Pain or no, Wilkins grabbed McLeane's shoulder

to pull himself up. McLeane helped him. The other Rangers had cut the parachute loose. Wilkins stood on one good leg, his arm around McLeane's shoulder, the bomb intact. He patted it like a baby. In the dark all of them could see his grin go from ear to ear.

O'Connor relieved Wilkins of his precious and very dangerous cargo. Barely able to walk for all his guts, Wilkins knew enough to pass the job on to someone else. With Wilkins hobbled the Rangers had to move slowly. But McLeane figured they could make the top, four hundred yards at most, in a matter of minutes. After that, they would take things as they came.

Four sentires could easily be seen in the clearing on top of Hill 457, and a machine gun facing due south stuck up over a well-camouflaged trench. McLeane and Contardo moved around behind the machine gun while the others positioned themselves where they had a clear bead on the sentries.

So far, Flagg's intelligence reports had been too right, and everything had seemed too easy. As soon as McLeane opened up on the machine-gun nest, the other Rangers followed. The silencers made muted, popping sounds, but some of the Japs fell with loud, agonizing groans which carried in the darkness and could have wakened the hillside.

One machine gunner turned on Contardo and McLeane and got off a couple of rounds before McLeane riveted him in the head with half-a-dozen shots from his 6.5mm. The sound of his skull shattering echoed throughout the hilltop.

"This is a piece of cake," Contardo whispered, glad for the chance to talk. With all the noise, keeping quiet made no sense. Besides, he had already set a record for not saying anything.

"Too easy," McLeane muttered.

Due west of the machine-gun nest, Wilkins sat against a tree with his bad leg out, grinning. He had taken out two sentries with only two shots.

"I've got to hand it to you, cracker," O'Connor said. "You do good work."

"Thank you," Wilkins said, unmindful of the pain in his leg.

"I don't like any of this," Heinman said.

The fighting stopped but the Rangers did not move. Instead they waited—waited and waited.

Then they heard a 7.7mm, and another. Then shots flew from everywhere. Wilkins calmly identified at least two 7.63 Bergman submachine guns, one Type 97 sniper rifle, and a lot of type 44 carbines.

"I guess they know we're here," Contardo said to McLeane.

"Lightly guarded," McLeane remembered out loud the words from Flagg's intelligence report. "Only a few sentries and one machine-gun nest."

For a moment the Rangers just listened, then they came up with the same conclusion. A patrol, come to check on the sentries, had walked into the Rangers. Actually, they probably had less idea of what was happening than the Rangers. They were firing with no clear idea of where the Rangers had positioned themselves.

With the Jap patrol at their backs the Rangers

found themselves in a poor strategic position. At the same time they had been in worse situations, and nothing serves so well as experience.

The flak didn't even come close to doing damage. Whatever the Japs used for anticraft couldn't shake a sparrow from a tree. The Catalina soared away in the night, untroubled. Corrigan patted the instrument panel and whispered a few sweet nothings to his favroite plane. Maybe he did care more about the Catalina than any woman he had ever known. She had certainly treated him better.

Corrigan had orders to wait. That meant fishing and lolling about in the sun and sleep. He did not want to think about the Rangers or the war until he next heard McLeane's voice over the radio. Corrigan pointed the Catalina toward Masini and opened the throttle.

Seven

A warm east wind blew off the Solomon Sea. For a moment the spray of Japanese fire had stopped, and the Rangers could hear the rustle of areca palm, baimolo, and banyan trees.

McLeane wanted a Chesterfield, but a cigarette would give away his position. Flagg's face crossed his mind, and he saw his fist smash it.

He lay down on a bed of maomori leaves. Ahead of him, a few Japanese bodies littered the clearing. To the right, even though he could not see it, the Japanese had dug a hole, an entrance to their stockpile of munitions. The Rangers had to get a bomb down there. He never believed Flagg's intelligence in the first place. Now he could forget it. Wilkins had a bum leg. In this kind of operation he needed every swinging Richard, and he needed him in one piece. In a short time the mission had become an even bigger question mark.

Next to him, Contardo sat coiled like a cat. Something in Contardo loved this kind of war.

On pure instinct McLeane fixed his bayonet.

Contardo checked his boot. He did not like a fixed bayonet. He liked the steel in his hand, the feel of direct contact as the blade slipped through the ribs.

Ninety degrees due east O'Connor had dug a hole, quietly, in which to put his perfect bomb. One shot into that hundred-pound black sphere and everyone within fifty yards would be apple sauce.

Wilkins had found a place under areca palms where he could hide and still see. His leg hurt like hell, but he said nothing. He had a new .45 automatic which he held and loaded carbine at his side. He reached over and fixed a piece of wood under his bad leg. By putting it up he could cut down on the throbbing.

A few yards away Heinman sat absolutely motionless.

No one spoke.

Heinman did not like the silence. With Jap fire power up, the Rangers could spot them. At that moment, in the deadly quiet, they had no idea if the patrol had left, moved in, spread out, or what.

Slowly, easily, McLeane turned around facing the jungle, his back to the clearing.

Contardo made a half-turn so that, taut and on the balls of his feet, he could move either way instantly.

Then the Rangers heard what sounded like footsteps coming through the brush—and voices. The voices and the footsteps came from everywhere.

Voices! Contardo thought to himself. What a bunch of amateurs! Any juvenile delinquent in Flatbush knows better than to make noise trying to do a job.

The Japanese had surrounded them.

McLeane saw shadows push out of the jungle. The Rangers lay hunched just yards below the Jap patrol. The Japs had to see them.

Suddenly, the air fell silent. The jabbering stopped. The shadows did not move.

McLeane waited a long moment, zeroed in on the outline of a person and then fired.

Contardo let out the Brooklyn war yell for which, at Ebbetts Field, he had become famous.

The Japanese screamed their best "Banzai!" and rushed forward from all sides.

McLeane opened up and knew he had hit two before another one jumped him. He saw a figure in the air above him, felt the vibrations of an angry voice on his face.

McLeane just held up his bayonet, felt the weight of the Jap soldier fall on it, heard the dull thud of the blade go up under his ribs. He twisted. The Jap let out one last sound. McLeane put his foot on a chest and gave the bayonet a quick pull.

A body, not quite dead, lunged at McLeane. McLeane felt hard fingers grabbing at his throat. He punched the Jap's face. A river of blood ran from the Jap's mouth onto his chin and stuck to McLeane's hand.

"This son of a bitch wants to take me with him," McLeane said, barely audible.

He gave the Jap a quick knee in the balls.

The soldier made not one sound, but hung on to McLeane's throat much harder.

Then the hands around McLeane's throat lost strength. McLeane reached the knife at his side. With one move he stuck the Jap in the back of the neck. The man fell forward, full weight, onto McLeane.

McLeane lay still. He wanted to catch his breath.

But he saw a hand come at him in the dark. He grabbed it at the wrist. The Jap died holding a knife.

He did not move for a while; then he eased the body onto the ground. McLeane wished he knew the soldier's name. If every Jap fought that hard, they wouldn't need weapons and the war would never end.

McLeane shook his head to get his wits back and touched the dead body next to him out of respect.

On the matter of respect Contardo had none, did not understand the word, had never heard it used. He knew only that two guys, very unfriendly, wanted to kill him and seemed very insistent on the idea. He had one on the ground with his boot pressed against the man's throat, and he had the other in a hammerlock. Contardo could not have been happier. No marine ever had more confidence. He had more fun making war than love.

"What am I gonna do with you two guys? Ya don't understand nothing. Ya gotta make trouble. Do I gotta kill ya?"

He waited a moment.

"I gotta kill ya."

For Contardo that was easy enough under most circumstances, but the Rangers could never comprehend why he always took so long to do it. Contardo loved the play, like a bullfight.

"Can you two slant-eyed cock suckers say 'Franklin Delano Roosevelt'?"

Without waiting he knifed the Jap he held in the hammerlock three times, first in the stomach and then twice in the kidneys.

"You can't say it either?"

He looked at the shadow on the ground.

Contardo kicked him swiftly in the groin; then he dropped down and stuck him under the chin. The soldier let out a groan.

"That is not how you say 'Franklin Delano Roosevelt.' "

Contardo turned to McLeane who had his hands full again.

"I think, sir, these Japanese people will never learn the ways of democracy."

Contardo could have been in his own living room. McLeane heard him out of one ear and marveled at his composure.

"Kill them, Contardo. That's all. Just kill them. This is war. Got it! War!"

Contardo kicked them both for good measure. "They don't get the 'Delano' right," he added. He saw the war as a matter of pronunciation.

The other Rangers had matters very much under control. Heinman had disarmed three sons of Hirohito single-handedly. He ran toward them as they rushed him on the principle that the best defense is a good offense. He grabbed the carbine from one as he kicked the other in the face. The third just froze. Heinman laid a rabbit chop into his stomach. The soldier dropped his weapon, fell to his knees, and started wretching. As an afterthought, Heinman knocked him out with a chop to the back of the neck.

Heinman body-blocked the one he had kicked in the face and tripped the one that used to have the carbine. The one that used to have the carbine fell on his nose. Heinman gave him a quick kick with the heal of a boot at the top of the spine. He heard a crack, then a loud whimper as the Jap shuddered and then was limp on the ground.

Suddenly, someone jumped Heinman from behind. In the dark he could see the flash of a knife blade. With a quick flip he threw the body over his head. It hit hard. Heinman could hear the thud. He saw the shadow of a figure flat on its back.

For a moment the figure did not move; then, before he realized what had happened, Heinman found himself stunned by a kick to the face. He could not see at all. He took a punch in the gut, then another. He doubled over in pain. A hard knee under the chin leveled him. He lay on the ground surrounded by black, unable to breathe. He opened his eyes to see something, someone flying on top of him. A single crack of a .45 automatic cut through the night. A body fell dead weight on top of Heinman.

"You owe me one," he heard Wilkins say in his easy, Georgia twang.

Wilkins, propped up comfortably and half hidden by the night and the brush, had been having fun shooting at those figures he could clearly discern as not belonging to anyone he knew. The recent Jap fatality, for example, had been noticeably shorter than

82

any of the Rangers.

Wilkins rather enjoyed this challenging, if risky, contribution to the war. Besides, he had such faith in his eyes and confidence in his marksmanship that he never really considered the danger.

"You damn near killed me, Wilkins," Heinman replied when he realized what had happened.

"Not a chance, Adolph, old buddy," came the cocky reply. "Give this ol' boy here a piece and only the bad guys need fear."

"Thanks," Heinman said, getting up. "But don't save me too many more times."

"You're safe as a virgin in a convent as long as I'm around."

Sometimes Heinman had doubts about Wilkins' mental stability.

At the point farthest East in the arc made by the Rangers around the top of Hill 457, O'Connor had been pistol-whipping an especially stubborn Jap soldier. The soldier refused to die.

"Die, you rotten son of a bitch," O'Connor spit as he pummeled the poor Jap first with the butt of his .45 and then with his fists.

He had already crushed the bone structure of the soldier's face, and his large hands pounded the Jap's features into pulp. Still, the Jap held on, offering minor resistance by grabbing O'Connor's throat. Finally, O'Connor just threw him down.

"Fuck this," he said out loud to himself. He turned the .45 on the bleeding figure and shot him twice in what remained of his head.

Earlier he had disposed of three Japs at once. They had been foolish enough to rush Chicago's surliest bartender in one of his surliest moods. He simply fired his carbine in the direction of their screams. "Banzai! Banzai!" They only said it twice.

Immediately, O'Connor checked the hole in which he had buried the precious bomb. Everything seemed intact.

That part of the job out of the way, the Rangers had only to lay down the bomb and beat it north to the coast. But they never thought that way. They just took things as they came, one thing at a time.

No one moved.

McLeane had taken out five Japs in all, Contardo three. Even Contardo could count that high. He only needed one hand.

"I'll get more next time," Contardo whispered, not ready to relax.

McLeane made his way to where Wilkins lay with his foot up.

"How's it going?" he asked in a low voice.

"I got two."

"I mean the leg."

"O.K. Throbs a bit. I wanted to get more, but I don't get around so good."

McLeane patted him on the shoulder and, keeping low, moved to Heinman and O'Connor who sat on either side of the bomb.

"What do you think, sir?" Heinman didn't know how to read the silence.

"I think we still have company."

"How do you know?" O'Connor seemed nervous. He had developed a personal attachment to the bomb he had made. It had become his child. At that moment, he worried about the bomb's safety more than his own.

"I don't know. Just a guess."

No one said anything.

"Watch this," said McLeane in a whisper.

He threw a stone into the clearing. It hit twice before a Type 97 machine gun opened up.

The Rangers lay flat. The gunner sat due south on the hill. McLeane figured he had two or three men with him. Since they had the big gun, he doubted they would go anywhere. He decided to wait and do nothing. None of them liked to wait, but they had learned how to do it.

On Vella la Vella Gen. Archibald Thompson sat in the canteen with Maj. Harold E. Flagg. Thompson had the eyes of a man into his second bottle of bourbon. He needed the coffee, or whatever they served instead, but he drank it like medicine. Flagg continued to look fresh, as though he had just showered and shaved. He had been working on a cup of powdered milk. He still had his clipboard.

"You always have to measure the odds on things like this, sir."

Flagg had been giving Thompson some deep philosophy. Thompson looked disturbed.

"I mean, really, we do an excellent job. Our sources are unimpeachable and our analysts the best."

Thompson pretended to listen.

"But there are always variables. A strong wind could come up unexpectedly."

"I'm worried about McLeane."

"Major McLeane knows these things, sir. He knows our reports are damn close to one hundred percent right. He also knows how to correct for a sudden wind out there. No, sir, I would not worry about Major William McLeane."

"Well, I'm worried about him."

General Thompson had begun to think that Intelligence might have sold him a bill of goods, and in the darkness, with silence all around him, he had begun to wonder if, perhaps, he hadn't bought it all too easily.

"Bill McLeane is the best soldier I know," Thompson said, narrowing his eyes at Flagg. "And those four men he has with him are not far behind."

"You don't have to convince me, sir." Flagg said, calling on his vast resources of sincerity. "I've known Major McLeane . . ."

At that moment, Pvt. Margot Thomas entered the tent. She did not see either General Thompson or Major Flagg, but walked directly to the large container of all-night coffee substitute and filled her canteen cup.

General Thompson, quite out of character, called to her.

"Private Thomas. Private Thomas . . . Margot!" He tried to get up, but decided against it.

She turned and calmly walked over to where the two men sat facing each other on long picnic benches over a collapsible table.

She nodded at both officers and said "Sir" twice.

"Sit down, Margot," General Thompson said. He was in an expansive mood. Anyone watching would not have recognized him. But he smiled for the first time all day.

"Please."

He held out his arm. Again he tried to get up, and again he decided against it. Margot tucked a few stray hairs under her cap and sat next to the general.

"What brings you out at this hour?" He sounded very paternal.

"I've been on duty, sir. It's 0013 hours. I just got off thirteen minutes ago."

"Private Thomas is a crack radio specialist," the general said, turning to Flagg.

"I know, sir."

Margot hated Flagg. She noticed the general's red-rimmed eyes.

"Hear any top-secret stuff over the waves?" The general made an awkward attempt at breaking the silence. She gave him a preoccupied smile.

"No. Nothing."

"Well, if you didn't hear it, then it wasn't there." The general patted her hand.

They sat alone in the sagging tent. A battery-run lamp shed a dim light where Margot sat with the general and Flagg. She did not look at them. No one said a word.

"Another cup of coffee?"

The general made the offer, but he still could not get up.

"No thanks, sir."

Margot looked at her watch. McLeane should have rolled the bomb down the munitions shaft by now and been off. She wanted to see him in a few hours.

"Do you think he's all right, sir?" Margot burst out suddenly. "Do you?"

She threw her arms around the general. He patted her on the back.

"I think he's fine. He's the best Marine in the Corps." Thompson looked at Flagg.

"The best," Flagg added quickly. "I would not worry about him Private Thomas."

General Thompson poured something from a hip flask into his cup.

"Combat's a funny thing," Flagg went on as if to no one in particular. "Anything can happen. It's important to plan. But even the best laid plans go wrong. Why, I can remember . . ."

Flagg noticed General Thompson staring at him.

Flagg shut up.

The improved Nambu Type II 8-mm pistol happened to be blowback and not recoil operated. Once again the information had been wrong.

Major Imamura could not sleep. Rather than flop around on his uncomfortable army cot, he decided to take apart and put together again the new model Nambu pistol Japanese military intelligence had given him before he assumed his mission for General Sasaki.

Very few had been made, Intelligence had assured him. He could count himself among the chosen.

Surrounded by tiny screws and springs and minute metal parts which otherwise seemed to have no purpose, Imamura muttered to himself, oblivious to events on another part of the peninsula. Lieutenant

Takata's voice returned him to reality.

"I saw you were awake, sir," Takata said, entering Imamura's tent. "I hope you do not mind."

Imamura smiled at the sound of English spoken.

"Please." With Takata, Imamura could relax, express the Western side of his nature, be American.

Takata offered him a cigarette.

"Thanks, I have my own," said Imamura lighting up a Chesterfield.

"I still like Camel," Takata said. "I'd walk a mile for a Camel."

They laughed.

"Do not let me take you from your work." Takata seemed very apologetic. "But I wonder. Are these Rangers so very good?"

"What do you mean 'so very good'?" Imamura had returned to his Nambu.

"Well, General Sasaki seems to think they are worth all this extra work."

"You really want to know if our commandos can take them when the time comes?"

"Yes, that is what I want to know."

"They have worked together a long time and are very courageous, not the way Japanese are courageous, of course, but courageous for Americans. And, like all Americans, they can be good in new situations." Imamura's voice trailed off as he held a tiny spring in his tweezers.

"McLeane, this major, he went to Columbia."

"Yes, he went to Columbia."

"Did they win the Rose Bowl in '34?"

"I do not remember if they won the Rose Bowl in

'34.''

"Did he play?"

"He was on the team."

"They played Stanford."

"Yes, they played Stanford."

Imamura seemed lost in reconstructing his new Nambu.

"I think Columbia won," Takata said finally. "I think they won 7–0."

Imamura nodded absent-mindedly, a gesture he learned from Professor Bojeczan, with whom he had studied differential equations at Princeton.

"Yes, yes, Lieutenant, perhaps they did win," he said. "But in combat we will take them."

Imamura looked up.

"And do you know why we will take them, Lieutenant?"

"Why will we take them, sir?"

"Because we are more disciplined." He spoke the words deliberately.

"Yes, sir, more disciplined."

They nodded in agreement.

Eight

The Rangers had been here before—behind a bush, in the middle of the night, pinned by machine-gun fire.

Contardo lay hidden directly in front of the gunner's nest. McLeane and the other Rangers found themselves ninety degrees to Contardo's left and due east of the Type 97 which periodically sprayed a wide arc with 8-mm shells just to make sure.

McLeane checked his watch. They would start to see light coming through the banyan trees in about two-and-a-half hours. Wilkins, with his bum leg, could move more easily during the day. On the other hand, they had a better chance of laying down the bomb and making it to the coast by night.

"How's the leg?" he asked Wilkins.

"It ain't no better."

At the faint sound of voices, the Type 97 laid

91

down a few rounds, but far away from any of the Rangers.

"Don't worry about that gunner," said McLeane. "He hasn't got any idea where we are."

McLeane knelt down in front of Wilkins' propped-up foot.

"Tell me when it hurts," he said, feeling from the thigh down.

His fingers pressed at top of the ankle, along the front of the leg, and Wilkins sucked in his breath. McLeane could feel the swelling. He wanted to take a look at it, but didn't dare strike a match or use a flashlight.

"Can you walk?"

"You're fucking right I can walk," Wilkins answered, offended that anyone should have asked. "And I can fucking run, too."

McLeane doubted both claims.

O'Connor had placed himself squarely over the hole which hid the bomb. He had decided to take any shot coming in that direction rather than let a stray bullet blow them all to bits.

"How's it look, sir?" Heinman asked McLeane.

"It looks like I'm going to knock out our friend over there." He pointed in the direction of the machine-gun nest.

"I'd better come."

"No, you'd better stay where you are."

"But remember, sir, you said he may not be alone."

"He is definitely not alone. That's why you stay here."

"You'll need help, sir, with the others."

"What makes you think they're there? What makes you think they haven't wandered out to look for us? What makes you think they won't come across Wilkins sitting over there with his feet propped up on vacation and O'Connor making love to a bomb?"

They heard a short blast from the machine gun, but did not see where it hit.

"Stay here, Heinman. I'll need you later."

McLeane dropped to the ground and, like a snake, moved through the jungle brush to circle in on however many of the enemy might be waiting for him.

Contardo enjoyed being alone. He liked the other Rangers, all of them, a lot, in fact, but at times he just didn't want anyone around. By himself he could think.

He had missed two baseball seasons. He did not really understand the war in the Pacific. No one had ever bothered to explain why America and Japan just happened to be fighting at a time when the Brooklyn Dodgers had such a great team. True, two years ago, the Yankees beat them in the Series. True, too, they did not look good going out in five. But Higbe and Wyatt both won twenty-two that year. The Cards took it all in '42, even beat the Yankees. Contardo liked that. The Yankees losing meant almost as much as the Dodgers winning. He wondered if Cookie Lavagetto would ever play again. He could get the scores late, but he could get them. But scores don't give the feel of the game. Reese had some good years left. The Yankees took it last year. They had Joe Dimaggio. Did Fitzsimmons still pitch for the Dodgers? All around, he thought Dom DiMaggio played better ball than his brother Joe. Other people thought that, too, but not a lot. Of course, the Dodgers still had Durocher. The Old Lip had to be the best manager ever, better than McGraw or Mack or McCarthy.

Suddenly, Contardo wanted to talk about baseball, see a game, go out to the park. He did not want to sit in the middle of some place he had never heard of before, surrounded by Japs who didn't know a knuckle ball from a rice ball. He bet not one Jap out there could make the throw from third to first.

Contardo got angry. He also wanted a good dish of spaghetti, with meatballs, the kind his mother made, and he wanted to sit around the dinner table on Sunday and eat it with his brothers and his sister and Uncle Vincent and Madeline from next door.

The machine gun cracked the silence again, this time with three short bursts and a long one that must have covered 120 degrees.

Contardo found himself very, very angry.

If Contardo liked being alone, he hated waiting, waiting and Japs.

Then Contardo got an idea.

Many positive things could be said for the soft, warm jungle floor. In nature, for example, McLeane doubted he could find a more comfortable place to sleep. Maomori leaves made a wonderful bed, except they left a reddish brown stain on everything, and McLeane had no desire to sleep anyway. McLeane did have a great desire to get around behind the machine gun that was causing everyone so much trouble. To do that he had to crawl, and for crawling the jungle floor could not be worse, especially at night. He kept getting sand in his mouth, he kept finding himself in holes, and he did not always like the strange little animals that ran across his face.

He stopped to get his bearings. He had left the Rangers exactly eight-and-a-half minutes behind him. In another five minutes he would be close enough to damage the machine gun. Meanwhile, he had not heard from it. In fact, the jungle had become unusually quiet.

He mounted his silencer, than heard the clear tread of boots through the brush coming toward him. The Japs had sent their noisiest troops to keep Hill 457, McLeane thought to himself. He supported his .45 across his left arm, pointed it ahead, and waited.

Soon the footsteps stopped.

McLeane continued to wait.

Nothing happened.

Suddenly, an excruciating pain shot up his right arm as a Jap boot came down hard on his hand. Another Jap rushed him from the side.

McLeane wanted to scream. Instead, he grabbed his carbine and unloaded it into the Jap who was rushing him. The man didn't know what hit him.

Above him, the dead Jap's friend fired his Nambu at point-blank range. McLeane felt bullets fly past his face. One grazed his right cheek and blood rolled onto his upper lip.

McLeane spun away, taking his would-be killer out with a kick to the knees and falling back onto the dead soldier. Blood poured out of the dead soldier's body. For an instant McLeane fogged over. In that long moment McLeane found himself face-to-face with what, in the dark, looked like a sword.

Had the Japs sent the cavalry? McLeane thought to himself. A sword meant McLeane had to be up against some kind of brass.

Now swords might be sexy, but McLeane knew they could be very unwieldy. Too heavy and too long. The son of a bitch swinging one could get tired before he killed anybody.

McLeane kept out of the way at first; then he began to move in on the man, like a wrestler waiting for an opening. In the jungle night McLeane found himself up against mostly shadows and occasional grunts.

After what seemed like a very long time, McLeane could hear heavy breathing. The sword came by less frequently, he noticed. The shadows stumbled.

This guy's knocking himself out, he thought.

For a moment the sword stopped, the shadows did not move.

Then suddenly, the Jap came at him, screaming. The machine gun opened up.

"What the fuck's going on?" O'Connor asked, not moving from his berth on top of one hundred pounds of explosives.

"I don't know," Heinman answered, his voice

96

worried.

"McLeane don't scream like that," Wilkins volunteered from under his arbor of areca palm.

"How did he know we didn't kill all the Japs there was?" The question had bothered O'Connor.

"The Japs have been sending out patrols of twenty. The major could only account for sixteen. Even if that figure weren't exactly accurate, you could still bet that a few were out there. Manning the machine gun, for example." Heinman always gave matter-of-fact answers.

"I guess he ran into some of them," said O'Connor flatly.

The Type 97 laid down a long barrage of fire.

No one spoke.

"That fucker's getting close," Wilkins said finally.

"Where's Contardo?" Heinman asked.

"He's over where the Old Man left him," said O'Connor.

Another flurry of machine-gun fire came too close for comfort. The Rangers had nowhere to go.

"Do you think he know's where we live?" Wilkins asked, already knowing the answer.

"Well, if he don't get us on the next couple of tries, they ought to send him back to machine-gun school." O'Connor hugged the ground a little harder.

The sword cut across McLeane's shoulder, tearing his shirt and leaving a large wound near his neck. But that did not stop McLeane from giving almond-eyes a solid knee to the groin on his way past.

The Jap dropped his sword and went down, clutching his belly and groaning.

McLeane had his knife drawn and, in one swift move from behind, struck him in the jugular. He hit deep, could feel blood gush all over his hand.

A relentless burst of machine-gun fire cut through the night, spraying bullets everywhere.

Suddenly, McLeane heard an explosion, one lone cry, then nothing.

He gave the knife a twist, pulled it from the Jap's neck, and headed for the place where he'd last heard noise.

Walking bolt upright, knocking branches away with his arm, holding his carbine ready, muttering, McLeane came upon the machine-gun nest in no time. A Type 97 barrel stuck up out of a foxhole covered by leaves, and over the foxhole stood the unmistakable outline of Corporal Contardo.

McLeane heard a single shot from a .45.

"I thought one moved," Contardo said.

"What happened here?"

"I threw them out third to first."

"What does that mean?"

"It means I got pissed off and decided to blow up these slant-eyed cocksuckers."

McLeane realized that more information from Contardo would not be forthcoming at that moment. No move was needed.

"Let's head back," said McLeane.

"Just a minute. I wanna make sure."

Contardo unloaded his carbine into the foxhole. They heard a final wretching sound.

"See what I mean, Major? You can't be too sure."

The two men headed back to the other Rangers.

Nine

War in the Pacific ignored the island of Masini during the summer and fall of 1943. The Japanese had come and gone by then, leaving the Allies free to use the tiny island paradise for this or that or nothing. After dropping the Rangers, Corrigan headed there to do nothing or something as close to nothing as possible—fishing.

He knew the island well and laid the Catalina easily into a quiet lagoon hidden by large asparagus and maidenhair fern and dendiki trees growing low along the shore. He cut the engines, let her drift, and then dropped anchor.

Rather than go ashore, he settled in the back of the plane, turned on the radio which picked up Darwin, Australia, if poorly, and opened a can of K rations. He had last eaten breakfast about twenty hours before, and the K rations tasted, if not good, better than he remembered. The radio made more static than music though he thought he recognized Harry James's trumpet. He left it on anyway, noise and all, leaned back, closed his eyes, and fell asleep.

Corrigan got up late and washed in the clear Pacific water that lapped against the pontoons of the Catalina. On the beach, he brewed a cup of ersatz coffee, which he drank with powdered milk, and heated a couple of dry biscuits from the bottom of K ration cans. He put two Hershey bars in his top pocket, grabbed his fishing rod and headed out across the island to where he had a hunch the bonita ran that time of year.

Masini, with long white dunes and clumps of jungle flora, occasional banyan trees, areca palms, ferns, and dendiki trees, belonged in a picture book. Corrigan saw animals which, until then, he had only read about: the birgus or coconut crab that came way inland to feed, bush hens, and the ground pigeon known as the Nicobar, with its bright colors and cocky strut. He even saw a couple of crocodiles slide into the only marsh on the island. If they didn't bother him, he wouldn't bother them.

He enjoyed the lazy walk in the warm sun to the narrow finger of sand that was covered almost entirely by wide-leaf areca palm. He pulled together a few pieces of driftwood and fashioned himself a kind of chair to lean against. Only a crazy man would try to catch bonita in the middle of a war. Corrigan felt crazy. He attached the bait—it looked like sand eels—he'd found lying around to his tin lure. On that part of the island the shoreline dropped off suddenly. Fish came within a few yards of the land. He looked around, cast beyond the reef, and then positioned himself in his driftwood chair.

Between intermittent bites, which amounted to nothing, Corrigan dozed. At one point he thought he might have something serious. He even stood up and reeled in the line, but the fish, or whatever, got away and he fell asleep.

How long had he been asleep? From the position of the sun he estimated an hour and a half. All the big ones got away. He looked out at the horizon. The glare off the water made seeing anything hard.

He could not be sure, but Corrigan thought he might have seen something foreign maybe a hundred yards off shore.

He stood up, shaded his eyes, and squinted.

He did see something foreign and more like one hundred and fifty yards away.

As well as he could tell, two, maybe as many as five, people seemed to be swimming to land. But at that distance and with the sun, he did not know if they were Japanese, American, military, or what.

He pulled his British Colt .455 and waited where the areca palm grew especially thick.

He didn't have to wait long until the swimmers came ashore. Even seventy-five yards off he could recognize five people. Two were definitely Western and definitely women. The other three were natives. He would read their gender later. Of the two women, one was a blonde.

He had gone fishing for bonita and caught mermaids instead. Corrigan smiled at his little joke.

Still, he did not go out to get them, but let them come ashore under their own power.

They rode in on what looked like pieces of a row-boat; and though they were obviously tired, they did not stop to rest, but started to run through the brush.

"Don't move," Corrigan said in his most cultivated Australian accent. He decided to give these women his best.

They stopped short. Fear registered in their bodies.

They had on very little. The two Western women wore nothing more than dresses and those were torn. The native women—Corrigan figured them for Gorai—had adorned themselves in the tribal loincloth and nothing more. Even from behind anyone could plainly see that they could not have been carrying weapons. To have frisked *them* would have been impertinent. Corrigan would frisk the Western women instead. In time of war one can never be too sure.

He ran his hand around the blonde's body.

"Is that really necessary?"

He moved to the other woman, who was slightly shorter and dark.

"Lay a hand on me, and I'll put you in traction."

Corrigan lost any desire he may have had to find out if she was armed.

"Turn around." At that moment those two words were all he could handle confidently.

The women turned around and put their hands down. Corrigan just stared. Maybe he had been away from civilization too long, but he could not remember seeing two more beautiful. The brunette had classic Italian features, the dark, piercing eyes, the straight nose and full lips, but the blonde, the blonde . . .

Corrigan fell in love with the blonde at first sight. She reminded him of every picture he had ever seen of the wholesome American girl next door.

She smiled at him.

"My name is Sally, and this is—"

The other woman stopped her.

"This is someone who is not saying another word until you put away that gun."

Corrigan did so at once.

"Sorry."

"And this is Anna," Anna said finally, smiling.

Their bodies relaxed. Corrigan noticed their full breasts and ample hips under the wet, white dresses. And Anna and Sally noticed Corrigan noticing.

"And these are our friends," Anna said pointing to the three native women who stood huddled together, terrified.

Corrigan could not keep his eyes off Sally. She had large blue eyes that seemed to look directly at him, lips that cried out to be kissed, and a body that would make Rita Hayworth hide in a closet and never come out. But he quickly got hold of himself.

"Let's get inland a bit," he said and led them to a small grove watered by a spring which seemed to come from nowhere. Sally and Anna lay in the shade of maidenhair and asparagus fern. The three natives stood together at the edge of the oasis. Corrigan tried to get them to move in closer, but the Gorai was suspicious by nature, he remembered. Nervous and totally smitten by Sally's beauty, he just hovered over the two women, looking his most brave and staring into Sally's ample cleavage when he thought she might not notice.

"I'm Captain Corrigan," he said finally. "I'm with the Royal Australian Air Force."

Sally wanted to know if his parents had actually christened him "Captain," but said nothing.

"I'm on a secret mission," he added.

With that comment Anna filed him in her head under *J* for jerk.

"Well," Sally began, "I'm Sally Lovett, and this is Anna Pucci. We're both nurses and both First Lieutenants and both wet."

They laughed. The humor escaped Corrigan, but he smiled anyway.

"How did you get wet?" he asked.

"Let me shorten a long story," Anna put in. "We found ourselves running guns to the Gorai who were running the Japs off New Guinea, and the Japs got us."

"Running guns?"

Corrigan had a hard time with women running guns. Men did that.

"I don't think we should get into that now," Anna said. "You ought to know, Captain, that we escaped from a ship not very far off shore. The Japanese might come back to look for us."

Corrigan had *more* trouble with this. How could women escape from the Japanese.

Sally noticed the questioning look on Corrigan's face.

"Please don't ask us to explain now, Captain. Isn't there something we can do?"

Briefly, Corrigan explained his purpose on Masini without giving away too much. In essence he told the women that even though he had to wait, his contribution to the war effort remained absolutely critical. He left them with the distinct impression that MacArthur and Nemitz both depended on him and required that he call in every hour. McLeane and the Rangers got little mention and then not by name. Afterward, Corrigan seemed rather pleased with his account of the war in the Pacific. Would the papers back home write it that way? Both Sally and Anna registered certain doubts which they kept to themselves.

At the thought that everyone might be hungry and in the absence of any bonita, Corrigan led his party of women back to the Catalina. In no time they came up over the rise which dropped down slowly to the lagoon where the plane lay safely hidden.

"I don't see any seaplane," Sally said, stopping to scan the land below.

Then he saw something.

"Hit it!"

Corrigan knocked Sally to the sand and brought the native women down at the ankles.

"What is it?" Anna seemed half annoyed.

Corrigan kept his eyes peeled to the left.

"Japs," he said.

A Japanese picketboat, guns forward and pointed slightly out to sea, sat harbored off shore. Out of the corner of his eye Corrigan had seen a party of Japanese moving cautiously inland.

Corrigan thought fast.

Among them they had a British Colt .455 automatic and some ammo, three grenades which he always carried for special occasions, and a fishing pole. Against a picketboat and a couple dozen well-armed Japs that left him on the losing side. A few hundred yards below, however, the Catalina waited, equipped with Browning 20mms and enough other explosives to blow a fleet of Jap battleships out of the water. The problem seemed to lie in getting to the Catalina safely and quickly with five women. If the Japs had not seen them, they would soon.

He had a plan.

"Directly below us, that is, about one minute and a half on a dead run straight down, is the Catalina." Corrigan spoke slowly and seriously to Sally and Anna. "When you hear a grenade explode, run like you never ran in your life. The plane is hidden by all the vegetation on the shore. Wait until I get there."

Corrigan had made two assumptions. First, he'd assumed that he had seen all the Japs actually on the island. Second, he'd assumed that he could take them out with three grenades and an automatic. If he hadn't seen them all or couldn't take them all out, he might as well kiss planet earth goodbye right then. Australians, however, possessed an outrageous belief in their own abilities. Living on an island surrounded by sharks can do that to people. McLeane called them arrogant. At the thought of McLeane, Corrigan smiled. He would show that cocky Yank bastard how to win the war.

He looked over at Sally with her beautiful, large breasts pouring out of her skimpy, white dress; leaned across to rub her back and butt with his right hand; and kissed her gently on the lips.

She looked astonished, then angry.

"Don't say a word, goddess of my dreams. That was for the war effort. I am now about to save your absolutely gorgeous ass."

He moved like a cat; then he turned his head back.

"Remember what I told you. Wait for the explosion."

He disappeared over a sand dune.

If he headed in the direction from which he had just come and circled around, Corrigan knew the jungle brush would hide him until he got behind the Japs. He just had to make sure he didn't lose them.

At that moment he could hear them. He took a quick look from behind a low-growing cluster of ansapo. He counted exactly six Japanese soldiers, all carrying 6.5-mm Type 44 carbines.

Corrigan had assumed all the enemy would stay bunched together so that he could hit them with one, no more than two grenades. They had, in fact, spread out slightly, almost into a fan.

He would have given an awful lot for a silencer.

But he kept with his original plan and eased himself behind the six Japs. By then, they had moved into the kind of V-formation used by the Rangers.

Corrigan had to bank on the element of surprise because he certainly did not have too much more on his side.

He checked his automatic and pulled a grenade, calmly standing exposed long enough to let fly with a shot at the number one man. He did not wait for a hit or a miss, but let fly with another shot on the left flank. Instants apart two explosions shattered four

Japanese bodies and caused a lot of screaming.

Corrigan hit the ground, getting sand in his eyes. He tried to let go with a third grenade, but couldn't see. Bullets hit around him. He rolled behind a banyan tree.

He knew he had hurt four Japs badly. He had no idea what had happened to the other two except that they were firing at him.

Suddenly, he heard Japanese voices running toward him. They wanted to gun him down at point-blank range. He let his last grenade go in the direction of the voices, turned, and just fired repeatedly with his automatic.

Blood splattered his face and clothes. The screaming stopped. Only the sound of his own automatic remained. He wiped his eyes.

A thoroughly mangled body lay three yards away, another right next to it.

Corrigan brushed himself off and walked to where the rest of the party struggled with or had already given up the fight to death.

A young enemy soldier, with his arms shot off and blood spurting out both sides of his body, looked up, terror in his eyes. Corrigan turned his head and shot him in the middle of the face.

Arms and legs lay scattered around the clearing. One body had a bleeding stump for a neck and no head.

Corrigan had no time to wonder why he'd managed to stay alive. He made another assumption. He had to assume that he could get back to the Catalina without running into any more Japs.

Ten

McLeane and Contardo found O'Connor still wrapped around his bomb and Wilkins still reclining regally under his arbor of areca palm. Heinman had been sitting and waiting.

"Glad to see you two chaps have come back," he said. "How many times have I told you not to stay out after ten?"

"O.K. Let's get this show on the road." McLeane sounded impatient. "We've got to get out of here before dawn."

O'Connor got up for the first time in a couple of hours.

"I thought you were gonna hatch that fucking thing," came a Georgia twang from under some areca palm.

The Rangers did not have time to make a sling for Wilkins. He would have to hobble down the north side of the hill on somebody's shoulder.

"How's your shoulder, sir?"

"Fine, Contardo, fine."

McLeane wanted a few moments to think.

Heinman touched his shoulder.

"What happened, sir? That's a nasty gash. Better let me wrap it."

"Later."

The stiffness on his left side had gotten worse, but he could still move his arm.

"Look, this has to go like clockwork."

Contardo had already found the entrance to the munitions shaft. They all moved freely at the top of the hill, abandoning caution for speed. If anything else should happen to them, they figured they could take care of it. Besides, Flagg's intelligence report, at this stage of the game already had them safely home.

They all huddled around Contardo.

"O'Connor, you and I will lay this bomb down this hole about five minutes after the others disappear through here."

McLeane walked over to a space between clusters of areca palm and maomori. It was large enough to be seen in the lifting darkness.

"The bomb will go off in seventeen minutes from the time O'Connor sets it. Contardo, you and Heinman trade off holding up Wilkins."

"I don't need no help."

"I don't need no help either, sir," said O'Connor.

McLeane said nothing, and the men knew they had spoken out of turn.

"O.K., you three, start moving."

Contardo grabbed a reluctant Wilkins under the arm and pulled him through the clearing behind Heinman. Heinman had his carbine ready. The other two had their automatics drawn.

McLeane hoped the extra five minutes would compensate for Wilkins' bad leg.

"O'Connor, let's go."

Quickly, they dug out the large round ball.

"This is a delicate piece of equipment, sir. I don't have to tell you—"

"No, you don't."

McLeane's shoulder hurt. If they dropped or let go of the bomb, everything would have been for nothing. Rather than roll it through too-soft earth, they lifted it inches off the ground and slowly made their way to the opening.

O'Connor wiped his hands on his pants. McLeane flashed a light on the clocklike dial on the face of the bomb.

"I'm setting this now. It will detonate in seventeen minutes. It may detonate sooner if it gets a bad bump."

"How accurate is seventeen minutes?"

"Plus or minus a couple minutes."

"What are the chances this thing won't work?"
The question hurt O'Connor's feelings.

"Close to none. It worked for the goddam Brits."

"O.K. Let's go."

They eased the bomb over the slight rise that circled the entrance of the shaft and let it go. They heard it drop.

113

Both men waited.

"I think she's O.K., sir," O'Connor said listening intently at the entrance to the munitions shaft.

The trip to the coast should take several hours according to Flagg. Given Wilkins' bad leg, McLeane added a couple hours to that. His watch read 0407. If all went well, they could be at the coast by 1400.

He radioed MacArthur's troops at division headquarters.

"Let 'em have it in five minutes."

McLeane looked around, just for good measure.

"Sir, we'd better get out of here."

The two men headed down the mountain.

Corrigan just jumped the last few yards into the clump of asparagus and maidenhair fern that lined the lagoon which hid the Catalina. He had run there flat out from the place where, minutes before, he'd massacred, single-handedly, half-a-dozen Japs. Someone must have seen him. On his way the picketboat opened up. But nothing scared Corrigan. Besides, the 155s were pointed into the air and away from him. The Japs on board had only small arms.

The women waited for him, hunched together and just a little bit afraid. They looked even more beautiful than he remembered. Even the Gorai ladies, not generally his type, began to have a certain allure. Still, Sally captured his attention.

"You all right?" he asked her specifically.

"Fine."

"We're used to this," Anna volunteered.

Corrigan wanted to take out the picketboat.

"You know how to use this?" He handed Anna his automatic.

"It's a British Colt .455, and yes, I know how to use it."

"Well, if you have to, do. I'll be back in a bit." He threw her a belt of ammo, and headed for the Catalina.

"Cocky little bastard, isn't he?" Anna loaded the automatic.

"He probably hasn't seen women in a while."

"He never saw you before."

"What's that supposed to mean?"

"It means he likes you."

"What do you mean 'he likes' me?"

"I mean, Sally, he wants to fuck your brains out."

They heard the Catalina start up and saw it move out of the lagoon and take off all at once.

"Well, if he touches me again, I'll break his hands."

"You're going to have to break something a little lower than that, my dear."

Whatever else they thought about Corrigan, they both agreed he had miles of guts. Through a clump of dendiki trees they watched him head out to sea.

"Where do you think he's going, Sal?"

"I don't know, but I'll tell you. He may be a jerk, but I think he knows what he's doing."

Corrigan loaded his Browning 20mms. The Rangers had also left some dynamite on board. Normally, he did not allow explosives stored on the Catalina, but at that moment, he wished he had more.

The picketboat had guns pointed north and south. Corrigan would hit them east and west. Even if they could turn the guns around quickly enough, they would never get them accurate in time to do him any damage.

He checked his instruments. Two miles out to sea gave him the distance he needed. He turned the Catalina around one hundred and eighty degrees and opened the throttle.

Excitement rushed through him as never before in the entire war. The Catalina picked up speed. He began singing "Waltzing Matilda" at the top of his lungs.

"Are you watching, Sally, you gorgeous piece of something good? You are witnessing the best fucking flyer in the whole fucking war. And when I finish blowing these bloody little Nipponese out of the fucking water, I am going to return to your loving arms and fuck you between the tits till we both go blind."

The Catalina came up on the picketboat.

"Do you read me, Sally? Right between the tits."

He dove for the picketboat and opened up with the Brownings. Coming low over the Japanese, he lit a bundle of dynamite and let if fly out the cockpit window. Rifle fire from on board missed him.

He took the plane up and turned her around again hard. He didn't worry about the big guns and would have to take his chances with anything else. The Brownings had done their work. He opened fire on them again and let them have it with more dynamite.

"This one's for you, Sally Baby!"

He turned around again, this time sharply at ninety degrees, and came at the boat from the north. The Japs had no idea what to do. Throwing caution to the wind, he flew so low, he could eyeball the captain on the bridge.

"Get those tits out, Sally."

He dropped two loads of dynamite directly on the ship. The Catalina shook from the explosion.

He made one more pass. He could see the boat smoldering. This time the Brownings did all the work.

"Are they out, Sally? Because I'm coming home."

Out of the corner of his eye, Corrigan saw a couple of enemy sailors jump ship.

He rendered a few more bars of "Waltzing Matilda," staying with the first verse, but picking up the tempo considerably.

He circled the now-burning boat several times for signs of activity on board; then he placed the Catalina in her berth by the lagoon.

He hopped out of the plane, strode through the water, and walked directly up to Anna.

"Let me have this."

He took the automatic and, without breaking stride, walked the beach to where the Jap marines lay on the sand struggling for breath.

"Here," he said. "Let me help you two chaps."

With that he blew their brains out and headed back.

Major Imamura held one final screw the size of his fingernail and to save his life could not figure out where it belonged. During the last three days, he must have reassembled his Nambu half-a-dozen times and each time one or another part remained. And each time he could not get the pistol to work.

Then a thought occurred to him. He opened the handle. Inside, behind the trigger a small hole hid under a metal lip. He could not see it too well, but felt it easily with a match stick. Carefully, using a tweezers, he dropped the screw into the hole. It fit perfectly.

His eyes burned from lack of sleep. The Nambu had become an obsession. This time it would work.

A few turns of the screwdriver and the screw sat snugly in place. Imamura checked the piece thoroughly. He loaded a clip and went outside to fire a round.

He sighted on a marker he had cut into a banyan tree twenty yards away.

He pulled the trigger.

Nothing.

He looked over the weapon very carefully, checked the barrel, examined the clip. Everything seemed in order.

He sighted on the mark again and again pulled the trigger.

Nothing.

He stifled the wave of frustration which threatened to overcome him at that moment. Instead of raging, he stood calmly with his hands at his sides.

Then, in one calculated move he threw the Nambu against the banyan tree, just below the mark, actually, he wanted to shoot. He did not bother to check his aim, but turned and went into his tent.

The Japanese would never win the war with weapons like that, he thought to himself.

Eleven

MacArthur's troops got anxious. McLeane and O'Connor barely made it off the top before they heard shells hitting the south side of Hill 457.

According to Flagg's plan this assault on the south side of the hill would leave the Rangers free to escape easily down the north side of the hill.

McLeane went over that a couple times in his head. So far, Flagg had been right enough. Would he really have to apologize to that four-eyed faggot? He hoped so. He did not like to think about even Flagg's plans going wrong.

The first light broke through the banyans and jungle shrubbery. Once able to really see, they could make their way more easily through and around the tangle of brush that lined the hillside like a rug.

McLeane's shoulder began to throb. He could barely move his arm and then only with great pain.

In the background the noise of artillery and gunfire became more insistent.

They could see the path the other three had taken. O'Connor wondered out loud how Wilkins managed such a steep incline. The sandy earth certainly did not help.

The tempo of the fighting behind them had really picked up.

"I guess they don't like each other back there," O'Connor commented, moving cautiously along a particularly questionable ridge.

It's only a three-foot fall, he thought to himself.

Suddenly, McLeane grabbed his shoulder.

For a second they both stopped.

They heard the same thing.

Not all the firing had been coming from the other side of the hill. No one could mistake the sound of 6.5-mm carbines in front of them.

"Our guys are trapped."

O'Connor wanted to run. McLeane felt a slow rage building inside him.

"First, just listen," McLeane said.

Sound does not travel as clearly in the jungle as in other places, but McLeane could still get some idea of where the enemy might be positioned.

"They're completely surrounded by, I would guess, twenty troops," O'Connor said.

"They're surrounded all right, but by thirty troops," McLeane corrected him.

"How do you know?"

"Trust me."

Isn't that an odd number?"

"It's an odd war."

They checked their weapons.

"Here, take these." McLeane handed O'Connor two grenades.

"Let's just go straight down as fast as we can until you see them. As soon as you see them, hit them with a couple grenades and take cover. That should give our guys a chance to move."

That is almost exactly what they did. O'Connor added a little embellishment. On seeing his first Jap, O'Connor let out a war whoop worthy of Contardo as he threw the first grenade. He threw the second right on top of the first and saw four bodies go up in the air and come down in pieces.

McLeane found himself suddenly faced with a bayonet. One young enemy trooper was behind the rest. He'd seen McLeane coming and, terrified, tried to stop him by holding up his bayonet.

"Oh, please," McLeane muttered. "I don't want to do this."

With his bad arm he swatted the kid away. The kid went sprawling, losing his rifle to McLeane. He had no weapon and nowhere to go. He just turned, got on one knee, and slowly put up his hands.

"I don't have time for this," McLeane said, holding the young soldier's rifle. He shot the lad between the eyes with his own weapon.

The young man's face froze in horror the instant the bullet impacted his skull.

McLeane shook the picture from his memory. This was no place for people under twenty-one. People over twenty-one weren't much better received either.

His watch read 0422.

In two minutes the bomb would blow and take the whole top of the hill with it.

In the last fifteen minutes he had heard a lot of Japs move over on the other side. He hoped the Rangers had made enough distance between themselves and danger.

O'Connor ran up to him, pointing at his watch. Neither one had an idea of how the other Rangers had made out. For a second the fighting had stopped.

McLeane turned and looked in the direction from which they had come. He could see the morning sky and the tops of the banyans coming together. The areca palm all ran together. He found himself, suddenly, overcome with exhaustion. They had been at this only six hours. He shook his head to clear the cobwebs. Everything closed in around him.

"You O.K., sir?"

"Don't ever ask me that again, and don't call me sir."

Then the mountain blew. The instant before the lights went out for him, McLeane heard the loudest noise he had ever heard in his life.

He opened his eyes to see the sky and the tops of a couple of banyan trees but not much else. He found himself on a bed of needles and leaves, covered over with branches of trees and shrubs he could not identify. He wiggled his fingers and toes. At least everything worked, even if all of it hurt like hell. McLeane turned his head to the right.

"My God!"

An entire mountaintop had been shorn away. The

shelling continued on the other side of what was left of the mountain.

MacArthur's troops sounded about two miles away. If the dumb bastards couldn't take Hill 457 now, McLeane didn't want to hear about it.

He tried to move the branches away. The wound on his left shoulder still hurt, but not as much as some of the rest of him. He kicked his legs. A branch from a kisu tree fell off. Kisu trees grew abundantly at the top of the mountain. He had not noticed any farther down.

From the light it had to be late in the afternoon. McLeane gave another kick, this time with both feet. But nothing moved. He stuck up his head to see bamboo lying like timber across his feet.

Amidst the firing he thought he heard footsteps coming toward him, the snapping of an occasional twig in the sand. But the heavy action on the other side made it impossible to know what might be happening for sure.

He figured that around this time he should have been calling Corrigan, if for no other reason than to ruin the Aussie's vacation.

Then a figure came on him out of the corner of his eye. He turned his head in an instant.

"I'll have you out of here in a second, sir."

"Don't call me sir."

"What's this 'don't call me sir' shit?"

Contardo stood over him with a grin that went from San Francisco to Saipan.

McLeane started to laugh, but laughing made his ribs hurt.

Then O'Connor appeared.

The two of them set about removing island flora from McLeane's buried body.

"Fifty yards farther up, sir," said O'Connor, "and we wouldn't have been here."

Despite the pain, McLeane just kicked and swung and threw and spit and cursed until four hands reached out to pull him up, get him vertical again.

"Where are the others?" were the first words out of McLeane's mouth on seeing the world upright.

"Everybody's fine," said Contardo. "Heinman is with Wilkins."

"What happened to the Japanese?"

"They died."

Contardo had a way with language. He led them to a snug bunker of low-growing areca palm and the stumps of banyan trees. There sat Wilkins with his leg on a pile of coconuts, his Smith & Wesson in his hand. Heinman knelt over Wilkins' leg.

"Take a look at this, sir." Heinman wore a very serious expression on his face.

McLeane fingered the swollen flesh around the ankle.

"You've got a broken leg, Wilkins and it's infected."

"Don't bother me none. I shoot with my hands and my eyes. I can still kill Japs as good as ever."

"They don't need legs in the south," commented O'Connor. "Alligators bite 'em off anyway."

"Well, he can't walk, and that's an order."

"We can make a stretcher or a sling," said Contardo, holding up strips of sensi leaf. "That's not hard."

"Good idea."

O'Connor and Heinman went off to find sensi, some larger areca palm, and some bamboo.

McLeane looked around.

"Well, Wilkins, we did the job."

Surrounded by debris, with the mountain-top collapsed into the earth, Wilkins had to agree.

"We done that, sir."

With Wilkins in a sling and no trouble, they could make the coast in six hours.

McLeane looked up to see O'Connor running hard through the brush.

"Japs," he said out of breath. "Maybe two platoons."

He watched the anger burn in McLeane's face and heard him mutter something about Flagg.

McLeane's watch read 1518.

On the island of Masini Corrigan checked his watch at exactly 1518. Almost eighteen hours before, he had dropped the Rangers. He could expect radio contact at any time.

After his brief confrontation with the picketboat, he had gotten the women aboard the Catalina. There they could rest, protected from the sun, and there, too, he could listen for McLeane's voice. He had gathered some coconuts and dates that lay in a tiny cluster of green on the other side of the lagoon. They would make a welcome supplement to the K rations that would be the main meal.

His major concern lay in another visit from Japs, so he stationed one of the Gorai women outside to keep watch. They could all rotate shifts.

Until further word, Corrigan and company had nothing to do but sit around.

"Maybe you ladies could tell me now," he said eating dates, "how you got here."

They sat opposite him on the floor of the fuselage, and Corrigan could not keep his eyes off Sally's cleavage.

"It really isn't complicated, Captain," Anna began. "We were running guns to the Gorai and got caught."

"Then we got away."

"Then you found us."

Corrigan just nodded his head.

"Happens every day." He smiled. "Now, let's start from the beginning again. You 'were running guns to the Gorai.' What does that mean?"

The women saw they could have fun with this. At the same time they wanted to be a little serious with the pompous Captain Corrigan.

"We have both been attached to the Allied Land Forces," Anna began again.

"As what?"

"As nurses." Anna smiled. "Be patient, Captain."

He wondered if they were pulling his leg. He wanted to rip off all of Sally's clothes and take her right there in front of God and everyone.

"We were originally sent over with the Sixth Division," Anna continued. "But actually before we got with them, we were transferred to Bramley's Land Force. They were suffering very heavy casualities and needed medical help badly."

"We were stationed in a field hospital run by

Australians in Tarakan on Borneo," Sally added.

"Yes, on Borneo," Anna went on, "and that's where I met Colonel Josephs."

Sally laughed.

"Met him? You had an affair with him."

"That's not the point, Sally."

"You were the talk of the hospital."

"I really don't think Captain . . ."

Sally clearly enjoyed teasing her friend.

"And you didn't even like him. No one liked him, and he was short and bald."

"Really, Sally."

Now Anna had begun to laugh.

"Come on. Get on with it," said Corrigan, getting increasingly more impatient.

"Short, bald, and nasty Josephs happened to run a covert special forces unit," said Sally still giggling. The Gorai hate the Japs and have been running their own private war against them ever since they landed on their island.

"Josephs had been trying to get arms through to them."

"But he couldn't," Anna interrupted. "His men couldn't get through the Japanese."

"So he decided to use women."

Of course, Corrigan had no faith in the ability of women to do anything that wasn't covered in the Old Testament, but he suppressed a need to guffaw. After going over the matter in his mind, he decided that he did not know Josephs, but that the man had to be a fool.

"Anyway," said Anna. "I volunteered for the job."

"And you volunteered me too."

"At first Josephs thought I had lost my mind. Then he reconsidered. We made three contacts with Gorai women before this last mission."

"Yes, Josephs thought no one would suspect women. And he was right, too, mostly." Sally had a need, it seemed, to always clarify the record.

"But what happened on this last mission?" Corrigan asked with growing impatience. He knew the Gorai lived on islands all around Masini. He also knew they had no great love for the Japanese. Asking him to believe that an Army colonel, and an Australian at that, really used a couple of women to run guns to them violated his most vivid imagination.

"Well," Anna went on. "It's really simple. We made a scheduled contact on Paki."

She pointed slightly south.

"It's so small it isn't on the map, and the Japs never go there. There's no reason for them to. Well, this time they were there, only three, but enough to confiscate our weapons and stop our operation."

"But how did you get there?" Corrigan had to get up and pace for this one. "I mean it isn't exactly as though boats go there every half-hour."

"We were dropped off from an Australian tramper. This time it was the *Matilda*. They put us in a speed boat."

"Anna drives a speed boat better than any man," Sally volunteered.

That comment did not set well with Corrigan. He had enough difficulty with women in uniform. He did not want to hear how much better they were than men.

"We were dropped off the *Matilda* in a speedboat with the weapons and ammunition. From there I drove the boat through the night to Paki.

"Two canoes of Gorai women waited for us."

"Where are the rest of them?"

"There were two canoes and four women. The Japanese shot one of them."

"How did they find you?"

"They were waiting for us when we arrived. I guess they just stumbled on the two canoes. They were on a bivouac exercise and found us. The Gorai tried to warn us, but we didn't read their signal."

"And how did you get away?" Corrigan continued to walk up and down the fuselage of the Catalina. He had to believe what they told him.

"We waited for them to fall asleep—they only left one guard and now he sleeps with his ancestors—then we slipped away in one of the boats. One of them woke up and discovered us gone when we were about one hundred yards off shore, he fired into the boat killing one Gorai and breaking the boat into splinters."

Anna stopped talking.

"Then we swam to Masini." Sally finished the story.

"Then you 'swam to Masini'" Corrigan repeated.

"And met you," she added.

Corrigan nodded his head.

"That's some story."

"That's how it happened, Captain."

* * *

Margot Thomas was halfway through the second shift when the news came over the radio. As tired as she may have been, the importance of the message knocked her right awake.

"Take over for me," she said to the radioman next to her and without waiting for a reply bolted out of the tent. Sand shifted under her feet as she ran to the canteen where General Thompson and Major Flagg would be having their morning coffee.

"Sir." She almost fell getting to General Thompson and had to catch her balance on the table where the two of them sat. She stopped to catch her breath.

"Sir, I've got to talk to you. It's important."

"Easy, easy." The general took her elbow as he got up. "What is it, Margot?"

"It's Mack, sir." She spoke confidentially so that no one could hear.

"Well, surely we can let Major Flagg in on the news."

"Of course," she said as Flagg presented his most serious face. "Mack did it. They blew the hill."

Suddenly, she started to cry.

"They did it, General. They did it."

Flagg smiled. "See, sir," he said.

Thompson had turned to Margot.

"Of course they did it, Margot. Of course, they did. They're the best marines ever. Now sit down and get hold of yourself."

Margot had dissolved into incessant sobbing.

Flagg and Thompson walked to the entrance of the canteen. They both read the radio report.

"That's all it says, General. MacArthur's troops

have already started to move."

"Let's hope they keep moving."

Thompson seemed obviously distracted and looked over at Margot.

"Is there some problem, sir?" Flagg asked.

"This is a war. There are lots of problems." His voice had taken on an edge that was unmistakable. Flagg decided to say nothing.

"This is why I don't want women in uniform."

"Sir?"

Flagg did not quite follow the general's thought.

"She's too involved with McLeane," he said, nodding in the direction of Margot. "I'm shipping her out for a week. She needs a rest."

"Of course, sir."

"You tell her." General Thompson put his hand on Flagg's shoulder.

"Any R&R station in the Pacific," he added and walked out of the canteen taking long, confident strides.

Twelve

"Give me a 6.5, my old Thompson, enough ammo to keep me alive a couple hours and leave me the fuck alone," Wilkins hollered. "I'm gonna shoot myself some Japanese asses."

The Rangers laughed at Wilkins' 1928A Model. They all used the newer model submachine gun made in 1942. But they had to admit he did things with the old one they couldn't imagine doing with the new one.

If McLeane was angry, the other Rangers seemed pretty calm.

"How are we fixed for grenades?" McLeane wanted an ammo check.

"Forget grenades," O'Connor said patting his backpack. "I've got enough dynamite in here to blow those Nips back to fucking Tokyo."

Carrying explosives in a backpack not only violated regulations, it also happened to be dumb. O'Connor, however, did have a special rapport with things that blew up. McLeane decided to chew him out later.

"O.K. O'Connor," McLeane said, standing in the middle of the clearing like a cop directing traffic, "as soon as you see the right flank come through the brush there, get rid of them any way you want."

"Yes, sir." O'Connor already had ten yards of fuse out, and he had more.

"You set, Wilkins?"

"Yep."

Heinman had already planted himself behind his own Thompson which he had put on a tripod. Contardo, with his fear of heights, found a low-hanging branch on an areca palm. He hid there well camouflaged and with a good view of things to come on the left.

"Now, I'm going to stand here and see that you do it right this time."

That one got a laugh.

"Fuck you," O'Connor yelled over his shoulder; then he added, "sir."

"Don't call me sir."

That one got a war yell from Contardo.

The first Japs to come upon the Rangers heard American laughter and saw a tall major standing in the middle of a clump of trees with one arm raised. They did not have long to meditate on the scene. Heinman cut them in half with one arc of his submachine gun.

Contardo picked off three of Hirohito's finest as

they tried to move behind the Rangers. He fired his M-1 so fast it sounded like an automatic.

"Maybe that Guinea's learning to shoot," Wilkins said out loud as he picked his shots. He took out two of the enemy, one in the left eye and the other in the right at sixty yards. Wilkins smiled.

"You're one hell of a shot you are," Wilkins congratulated himself. Making that hit at that distance was like catching a marlin with a fly rod. Wilkins loved himself. He'd done it with an automatic. General Thompson couldn't do that that with a scope on an M-1.

The Rangers were loose.

"O.K., guys. Here goes."

O'Connor waited for the Japs to move closer on the right flank before lighting a fuse. Then he ran.

"Hit it!" he yelled at McLeane, and the two men dove just as everything went into the air.

When the thunder died down, McLeane raised his head. O'Connor had blown a line fifty yards long, but nothing on the side of the line where the Rangers had settled in got damaged.

"How do you do it?" McLeane looked over at O'Connor.

"Genius, Mack. Genius."

At that moment a grenade hit about twenty yards in front of McLeane.

"Next time they won't miss. Let's get out of here." Instead of taking cover on the right, which O'Connor had cleared out with his dynamite, McLeane went straight up the middle toward the Japs, laying fire all over from the Thompson at his hip.

O'Connor didn't believe what he saw. "The

guy's fucking nuts,'' was all he could say.

For some reason, suddenly, to McLeane every Jap looked like Harold D. Flagg, Major, Intelligence, and he wanted to smash that man with his fist, the butt of his weapon, anything.

He was like a man gone mad.

One Jap saw him coming, dropped his weapon, and started running. McLeane threw his sub away and brought the Jap down from behind, a move that took him back to his days on the Columbia football team and made him feel good.

The Jap had no chance.

McLeane pinned him with his knees and pummeled his face to a bloody pulp. When he'd finished, the Jap had become unrecognizable, and McLeane's shoulder did not hurt so much anymore.

He took a second to view his work. With his cheekbones completely caved in, the poor Jap could have been anybody. McLeane imagined Flagg beneath him and took one more hard shot with a right where a nose used to be.

Another Jap jumped him, but McLeane employed the basic judo flip, and little Hirohito went sailing through the air. Still one more Jap tried the same thing and received the same treatment, landing directly on top of his friend.

Now, confronted with two Japs, McLeane lunged at both, grabbed each by the collar, and smashed them together.

A stream of high-pitched Japanese followed.

He smashed them again.

Action on the right had stopped completely since O'Connor had blown everyone away. Action on the left had slowed down. The Japs sent a final suicide wave which Heinman and Contardo finished off. Two Japs got through, but O'Connor turned them into hamburger, and Wilkins picked off a would-be sniper before he could get snugly into his tree.

"Shall I, sir?" yelled Wilkins, wanting to shoot a couple more Japs.

"Don't get greedy! These are mine!"

McLeane gave one a boot right in the middle of the gut.

"Never saw the Old Man having such a good time," O'Connor said to Heinman, still pointing his carbine toward the jungle.

McLeane had the other Jap in a hammer-lock so tight that the man's feet left the ground as McLeane swung him around. Then, with one expert twist of the arm, the Jap's neck snapped. McLeane let go, and the soldier's limp body fell to the ground like a rag.

Suddenly, McLeane found himself on the ground, a pair of hands squeezing his throat. He pushed up against a face he could not see and hooked a thumb inside an eye.

The Jap screamed and fell away. McLeane found an eye on his thumb and fresh blood on his fatigues.

Even in excruciating pain the Jap would not quit. He went for his knife. McLeane kicked it out of his hand, decked him with a clean left hook, and connected with a right going down. Joe Louis would have been proud of him.

The Jap just lay there.

"We're taking no prisoners today," said Mc-

Leane. He calmly reached down and snapped the Jap's neck.

"This is my week for breaking necks."

Contardo applauded from his perch in the areca palm.

"Good one, sir."

Tired, but feeling better than they had in a while, the Rangers gathered around what had come to be known as Wilkins' hospital bed.

"Well, I thought we wasn't supposed to see no Japs this side of the mountain." Wilkins knew he had hit a sore spot.

"That's what Major Flagg said, isn't it, sir?" O'Connor wanted in on the act. "No Japs over here."

McLeane gestured vaguely toward the jungle.

"Let's make that stretcher for Wilkins and get the hell out of here."

The less said about Flagg the better.

Corrigan had replaced the Gorai woman on watch and had walked his post alert to the sights and sounds of the island. His thoughts, however, remained inside the Catalina with Sally. He wanted her desperately.

Sadly for Corrigan, she did not want him at all.

"He's good-looking," she told Anna, "and kind of sexy, but I can't stand anyone that stuck on himself. He's so conceited."

"Well, he'll be coming back on board any minute now, and it's my turn to pull guard. Will you be all right alone with him?"

"Let him lay one finger on me, and he'll have to

140

put his crotch in a cast.''

Normally, Sally never talked that way. On this matter she had strong feelings, Anna thought.

''Here he comes, kid. You're on your own.''

Corrigan climbed into the plane and gave his .455 automatic to Anna who checked it and disappeared. He walked the length of the fuselage to the instrument panel and turned on the radio which he had forgotten to do. He took a long drink from the bottle of distilled water by the pilot's seat and returned to sit opposite Sally.

She pulled an army blanket over her shoulders.

''It gets chilly here at night.''

''Yes.''

In her presence again he didn't know what to say.

''I guess we took care of those Japs this afternoon,'' he said finally.

''You did all the work, Captain.''

''Yes, I did come to think of it.''

He cleared his throat.

''I enjoy my work.''

''That's clear.''

''I've been flying a long time. Some people think I'm the best flyer in the entire Australian Air Force. They may be right, I don't know. But I very much like killing Japs. It gives me a sense of accomplishment, a feeling that I'm doing something for somebody, my part, if you know what I mean?''

''Yes, I know what you mean.'' Sally turned her head away slightly.

''I'm waiting to hear from McLeane. He's the reason I'm here on this island. I dropped him and the Rangers.''

He stopped short.

"Well, it's over now. I guess I can tell you. We had a secret mission. I had to drop them by night on Huon. It's all Japs on the near side. I had to fly in at night, cut my engines, and glide. Not too many blokes can do that. I fancy I'm the only one in these parts. Now I'm waiting to pick them up. I don't imagine that will be too easy either. But we'll do it. You're safe with Corrigan."

He leaned over to pat her leg, but found himself palming the Catalina floor through an empty blanket.

"And, of course, with the Catalina here."

He recovered quickly.

"She's my baby. She's my wife and all my kids."

"You sound like you're very fond of her."

"Well, I spend more time with her than with anybody, and she's been very good to me. I don't know what I'd do if anything happened to her."

Corrigan could not remember ever talking so much. The sound of his own voice had come to bother him. Sally rolled up in the quiet as if to sleep.

"Listen, if you're tired, I can pull guard for you."

"No, I'll be fine." Sally raised her head. "Just tell me when." And she put her head down again.

Corrigan got up to fuss with the radio. Nothing came in too well. The way he felt, he could not have cared less if he never heard McLeane's voice again. The three Gorai lay huddled together behind the co-pilot's seat.

"Have you ever heard of McLeane and his Rangers,'' Corrigan yelled back. When Sally did not answer immediately, he went to see if anything might be wrong. She pretended she'd been asleep.

"Did you say something?"

"Sorry, I didn't know you were asleep."

Sally just looked at him.

"I wanted to know if you had heard of McLeane and the Rangers."

"No." She put her head down again.

"Well, you'll meet him. They're good, the Rangers, and so is he," Corrigan said, walking back to the cockpit. "Very good, in fact. But not as good as he thinks he is."

He stopped and looked back at Sally.

"And not as good as I am."

Sally only wished that she could sleep.

Major Imamura had been rousted out of bed and made to stand at attention for nearly half an hour in General Sasaki's private quarters before the general himself stormed into the room. He did not acknowledge Imamura's presence but, instead, paced up and down behind a Western type desk made of Philippine mahogany, screaming and smashing a pointer against a portable blackboard on which nothing at all had been written.

Imamura got the distinct impression that he had done something wrong, though what, he could not imagine. His men had performed admirably. If anything, they were overtrained. Only yesterday Sasaki and the Sixth Army High Command had watched them work out and bestowed upon every one of his commandos the highest accolades.

He could not be accused of oversleeping or over-eating since he seldom ate and rarely went to bed. He had followed every order given, even successfully anticipating a few for which he'd received a written citation as an officer in the Emperor's army worthy of the rising sun. No, in the early morning light, listening to Sasaki go on and on, the state of Imamura's mind was confused.

Then out of the screaming, Imamura recognized the name *McLeane*. The Rangers had been up to something. But Sasaki took time to say what exactly. When Imamura finally did figure it out, he smiled. On the one hand he had to hate McLeane. On the other hand he had to admire guts. These guys had guts, he thought to himself. He knew he could take McLeane, and he would for the glory of Japan, but he hoped he would have a chance to first shake his hand.

The general, chalk in hand, described, in detail on the blackboard, more or less what had happened on Hill 457: the entire mountaintop collapsed, MacArthur's troops were well on their way up the island, and the explosion killed an estimated 350 Japanese troops. With the mention of 350 Japanese troops General Sasaki stood directly behind the Philippine mahogany desk, pulled his sword, and nearly smashed the desk in half. He took a moment to regard his work and stormed out of the room. Imamura, a student of Western culture, wondered what had happened to Oriental inscrutability.

As soon as Sasaki left, his aide-de-camp, Col. Ishu Yamamoto entered, giving Imamura no time to relax. In a voice that could shatter glass Yamamoto screamed that the enemies of Japan and the Emperor should be destroyed at once and suffer the worst possible death and that Imamura would receive orders soon. Since he, Imamura, was the only person in the room, he wondered why all the yelling. As his friends at Princeton might have said, he was not sure he wanted to work for these guys. He did not voice this opinion, however, but bowed appropriately until Yamamoto left; then he withdrew himself to await further yelling.

Thirteen

The Rangers managed to reach the coast by nightfall. McLeane's shoulder had gone numb, and Wilkins' leg throbbed worse than ever now and without relief. Otherwise, the trip down had been uneventful. They could hear shelling and fighting behind them. The Americans had taken over, but the Japanese kept coming. McLeane no longer relied on Flagg's intelligence report—if he ever had. He knew that Japs could turn up anywhere, attack anytime.

Meanwhile, he had been trying to contact Corrigan. The Rangers had found large clusters of asparagus and maidenhair fern to use as camouflage. But that part of the beach sat exposed to the ocean, and every minute worked against them.

In the distance enemy aircraft came in off the peninsula, and unfriendly boats monitored the coast.

Contardo and Heinman had taken up watch at opposite ends of the beach. McLeane went out to check the area immediately behind the camp. O'Connor kept at the radio while Wilkins complained.

"Get Corrigan on that thing yet?"

O'Connor did not answer.

"He better get his ass over here because I ain't sitting here for the rest of the fucking war."

Wilkins sat with his leg up. He sighted down the barrel of his M-1 at lights flickering in the night.

"You see them fuckers out there, Irish? Well, they are gonna find us if we sit here long enough, and if they find us they are gonna shoot our ass. Now that could be lots of fun because then we get to shoot their ass, and shooting ass is about the best thing you can do with it. But we ain't got all that much ammo left."

O'Connor spoke softly into the radio.

"If you can't get Corrigan, try reaching that numbnuts, Flagg, why don't ya? Tell him to get his candyass out here. He's the one with all the news, all the *in*-telligence, and all the plans.

"Shut up."

"Or if you can't get him, there's always that other asshole, Thomp—"

"Whose side are you on?"

The tide washed in gently.

"Soon we're gonna get fucking wet if that fucking Aussie don't get his fucking ass—"

"Wait a minute."

Wilkins kept quiet. O'Connor thought he might be getting through.

"Can you read me? Can you read me?"

O'Connor put down the phones.

"I can get something," he said to Wilkins. "But I'm not sure . . ."

They both looked up to see McLeane push through the fern, holding a carbine at his side. They could tell by his step that he brought bad news.

"How're we doing?" he asked O'Connor.

"I've got something, but the static—"

"We've got company, Wilkins."

"Of course, we got company, and I'm gonna shoot off their asses."

"What's up, sir?"

"We've got company, but keep listening. They're a while away."

He headed to find Heinman.

"But they're coming," he added walking slowly away.

O'Connor worked frantically at the radio. Wilkins pulled his old Thompson across his lap and filled the clip. He had loaded his Smith & Wesson earlier. Wilkins felt good and ready.

Corrigan made sure he had all the information before he signed off and fired the engines of the Catalina.

"Ladies," he said to the three Gorai still huddled behind the copilot's seat. "You are now about to see Corrigan in action, a beautiful sight to be hold."

He raced the Catalina to the nearest clear area on the ocean, slowed down, reved the engines high, then took off at a forty-five-degree angle with the world.

" 'Waltzing Matilda, waltzing Matilda; You'll come a-waltzing Matilda with me, and he sang as . . .' "

Sally and Anna got a sudden rush of excitement. Why they did not know? Certainly, life had been full of greater thrills for them in the past. In fact, nothing imaginable could get their blood running faster than the thought of having been captured only forty-eight hours earlier by three Japanese.

"I want to meet this McLeane," Anna said after they had been up in the air a few minutes.

"Well, I don't." Sally curled up further into her blanket. "I'm tired of this war."

"I still want to meet him," Anna said a few minutes later.

"Now let me tell you what I've got to do, ladies," Corrigan screamed from the cockpit. "This is all highly technical and requires an enormous amount of skill. Not too many blokes can do this if I do say so myself.

"The Rangers have given me the coordinates of where they are on the map. But just to know the map isn't enough. You've got to know the actual territory. Personally, I know these islands better than the natives who live here.

"For example, we are going to land on a very exposed side of the peninsula. That means the enemy could see us easily even if they couldn't hear us. We are sitting ducks as you Yanks say. Now no map tells you that. But Corrigan knows it.

"Now what we've got to do when we make our approach is cut the engines and turn out the lights of this here baby and glide, ladies, glide.

150

"And that's tough, ladies, really tough. It's hard to control the Sweetheart here without the engine going and it's hard to see without the lights. But—and this is the important part of the message—have no fear because Corrigan is at the controls to assure your perfect safety throughout the remainder of the flight."

Sally put the blanket over her head.

"He is kind of funny, Sally." Anna smiled. "Anyone that stuck on himself is always good for a few laughs. I mean he is ridiculous."

The Catalina moved directly and at full throttle toward the spot on the Huon peninsula pinpointed by the coordinates on the map in front of Corrigan. After a few minutes, he turned to his passengers.

"In a second I'm going to cut the engines on my beauty here. When I do, I don't want a word out of you birds."

"Listen to who's talking," Anna muttered.

"I just want you ladies to sit in silence and watch in wonder as I perform miracles, ladies, miracles. I shall also ask you to remember and appreciate that you are witnessing the finest flyer in the whole bloody skies."

Sally refused to come out from under the covers. "O.K. Cut it."

Suddenly, the engines went out. The seaplane floated in the sky like a huge elephant. As Corrigan dropped the Catalina he could see an occasional light flicker on the ground and in the ocean. He had to keep his eyes peeled on the air in front of him, alert for enemy fighters that might cross his path or spot him. He doubted the women behind him knew how tough a job he happened to be doing at that very moment.

Slowly, quietly the Catalina approached the Rangers without incident. The closer it came, the more Corrigan heard gunfire. Instantly, he feared for the plane. A bullet anywhere in the Catalina, especially in a pontoon or through the supports that attached the pontoons to the wings, and she might sink. A hit in the engine and she might not start again.

He made a perfect landing on the water. The force of the water against the pontoons slowed the plane to just the right speed, and the Catalina coasted within a few yards of the beach before stopping.

The sound of gunfire had grown intense. Corrigan motioned to the women to stay in the plane. He put up his automatic, strapped grenades on his bandolier, harnessed his funny-looking Owens and dropped into the water.

He moved along the coast, keeping low, and then cut in toward the beach. He hit the sand chin first. He noticed the Rangers in a kind of arc with their backs to the ocean.

Everything went quiet.

McLeane saw the outline of the Catalina over his shoulder. This had to be the most snafued getaway in the history of warfare. If they made a break for the Catalina each and every Ranger would be sliced in two by Jap fire. If the Catalina stayed just off the beach much longer, the Japs would blow it. He wanted to wait until the coast got clear to call in Corrigan. But when would that be? He wanted to go after the Japs. But when would that be? He wanted to go after the Japs. But where were they and how many? He had Wilkins on his mind. The kid could not move, and he would not sacrifice him to any risky escape. As McLeane saw his chances, he could either wait indefinitely or hope for an opening and go for the plane. Whatever happened, he figured Corrigan would get involved, grudgingly, but actively. However little love may have been lost between himself and the Rangers, Corrigan could not resist the opportunity to show off, and he did love a good fight.

The enemy opened up again. Their fire had come from closer in. McLeane read their tactic. They would fire, stop, move in, fire, stop, and move in until they either shot the Rangers at point-blank range or tried to take them in hand-to-hand combat. At least he had been able to get a bead on not more than a dozen weapons, probably sentries left to guard the coast.

The firing had stopped again.

McLeane could not just let the Japs circle in and swallow the Rangers up.

He knew the position of each of them. Contardo lay ahead due east, followed by O'Connor. Heinman held down the other end of the arc. Wilkins sat somewhere in between with his foot up and, knowing Wilkins, three different weapons ready to fire in any direction.

Barely moving, McLeane removed a grenade, pulled the pin, and lobbed it down south, back, the way they had come, into the jungle. When it hit seconds later, a dozen Jap carbines let go at the explosion. McLeane opened up on as many as he could get with his Thompson before a knife went into his shoulder, his left shoulder. He wanted to faint from pain. Instead he simply reached behind, grabbed a shirt, and with just his right hand, threw the Jap over his head.

The Jap, stunned for a moment, came at him from the ground. At that moment he realized his left arm had gone dead. He could not lift it.

The Jap took him to the ground, knocking his Thompson away. McLeane lay there with small, iron fingers strangling the life out of him. He brought a knee up into the Jap's lower belly. That only made the Jap squeeze tighter.

He gave him another shot with the knee. This time, however, when he brought up his leg, he grabbed the bayonet from his boot and with one desperate lunge tried to knife the Jap in the neck. But the Jap moved, and McLeane's bayonet tore into the Jap's cheek. McLeane twisted, tore up, under the roof of the mouth, then down. Then the knife opened into the Jap's throat, and McLeane knew he had him. He felt the body fall off him, heard gasping sounds. He had cut an artery, and his enemy would drown in his own blood.

The Japs had come out into the open.

Two jumped Wilkins before he knew what hit him. He could not use his weapons and he could not move effectively. He could still cuss, however, and every chance he got he reassured his wrestling companions that they were a couple of "slant-eyed motherfuckers."

In one swift move, Wilkins deftly took a Jap in a

154

hammerlock across his lap while the other Jap, mistakenly, stabbed his partner in the back. That gave Wilkins all the chance he needed to knock the knife from the man's hand and, using the collar of his own fatigue shirt, choke the Jap to death.

Farther down the beach, Heinman had subdued one Jap with his foot. On his stomach, face buried in the sand, he suffocated struggling to get away from the heel of Heinman's boot while Heinman slit another Jap the length of his stomach. The Jap had come at him, but Heinman turned only slightly, like a bullfighter, enough to miss the rushing blade, enough to stick his adversary on an angle just below the breastbone. He ripped the Jap's stomach open. He could feel the guts and blood on his hand as the Jap died leaning on the knife.

O'Connor and Contardo had the brunt of the attack on the east side of the beach. Half the Jap squad, six men, rushed them in a suicide wave. The Japs fought a lot of the war that way. Sometimes they were able to overwhelm the Americans, but not often and never the Rangers.

Contardo and O'Connor would have felt safer in foxholes, but who had time to dig foxholes? Instead, they just stood their ground when the Japs came. O'Connor swung his M-1 like a baseball bat, connecting with faces.

"Here goes another one out of Comisky Park." A White Sox fan, O'Connor never discussed baseball with Contardo who, only a few feet away, was pulling another one for the Dodgers.

"You need help, Ginzo?"

"Fuck you."

Contardo loved few things in this life more than a stand-up slugfest. But going against three Japs he found no challenge. They screamed, rushed, bit, and scratched, but in the end, Contardo swatted them like flies. He took a bayonet off one Jap, snatched a 7.7 carbine from another, and just knocked out a third with a boot in the face. He then boxed the first two.

Even in the dark that presented no problem for Contardo. He jabbed one with his left and the other with his right. Then he would go after one of them with both hands, stop, and go back to fighting both of them again. In this way he managed to wear them down. He never wore down. In this way, too, he managed to prolong the fight and, therefore, the fun.

He landed a clean right to the nose, and the Jap on his right went down. He squared off on the other Jap and, with a flurry of hooks, beat him into unconsciousness. He took out his automatic and shot the three figures on the ground, as well as he could see them, in the head.

"There," he said, wiping his forehead with a sleeve. "That should fix the fucking Japs until their fucking cousins come through the fucking bush again."

O'Connor stood by his side.

"You like that word don't ya?"

"Shut the fuck up."

Shelling had been going on all night, first behind the Rangers from the south and then from behind them at sea. So they did not notice that the shelling from the ocean had gotten worse. When they finally sized up their situation, they realized that shells were hitting all around them. They headed back toward McLeane.

McLeane had moved out of the brush toward the water to find Corrigan lying face down on the beach.

"Hiding, Corrigan?"

"I came to save your fucking asses," he said getting up and dusting off the sand.

"Well you were very effective. I'll mention that to Thompson. All of Australia can celebrate your indispensable war effort."

Corrigan said nothing, just burned.

"Do you see that, Corrigan?"

McLeane pointed to the sky over the Pacific.

"See what?"

"All that flak and all those shells exploding out there?"

"Of course I see that."

Corrigan's voice had taken on the kind of irritable edge that always made McLeane smile.

"Unless you're crazier than I think, Corrigan, that noise out there and all those fireworks mean we shouldn't go anywhere."

"Clever, McLean, clever."

Except for Wilkins, all the Rangers gathered around.

"About two hundred yards past that bend, the brush has grown out into the water. We can pull the Catalina over there, hide her, and wait until things clear."

Corrigan said nothing, but started, with Contardo and O'Connor, toward the plane. Heinman slung

Wilkins across his shoulder and followed. McLeane headed out to check the coastline.

General Thompson had walked around and across Vella la Vella both ways before returning to the canteen.

He had much on his mind. On the one hand he felt good about the apparent success of the mission. On the other he felt bad about McLeane. He had an uneasy feeling that, even as he sat there drinking coffee, the Rangers were in trouble somewhere on the Huon peninsula, that Flagg's intelligence may not have been all that smart.

As he thought of Flagg, the major himself came into the tent, carrying his clipboard. He sat opposite the general.

"I talked some more with Private Thomas."

"Was that necessary major?"

"Well, sir, I thought a few words might help her feel better. She did seem upset."

"And?"

"Well, I think she feels better now."

Thompson tried to imagine Flagg consoling Margot. He did not want to know what the major had said. Margot disliked Flagg almost as much as McLeane did.

"Well, I want her out at dawn, Flagg. She's a dear lady and a good marine, but she's lost it, and I don't want her around when the Rangers get back. I don't want her upsetting McLeane."

"I'm sure she'll understand, sir."

"Did you tell her she's to be out by dawn, Flagg."

"Well, I told her she would feel better after a rest."

"Did you mention her shipping out at dawn?"

"Not exactly, sir. But I'm sure—"

"Tell her exactly, Flagg."

The Major left the tent without a word. The general wanted no misunderstanding.

Fourteen

McLeane stood in water up to his knees, guarding the Catalina. An overgrowth of areca palm, dendiki trees, maomori, and damiola made excellent cover. Corrigan insisted on keeping McLeane company, but then, after a few hours in the open, joined the Rangers inside the plane. He said nothing of his female passengers. McLeane hoped everyone could get some sleep. His left arm hung dead at his side.

The coastal shelling had almost stopped, but the air war had grown even more intense. The sky looked like any enthusiastic Fourth of July back in America. The American P-40s, the famous flying tigers, were going at the Jap Zeros. The Zeros had the tigers outnumbered, but from the sound of things, the tigers seemed to be winning. McLeane thought he heard an occasional Jap Tony. The Japanese had just come out with the Tony, and McLeane thought it a better plane than the Zero. The Japanese used it only for high-altitude fighting against the B-29. McLeane heard a couple of B-29s up there. The Tony had a lot of maneuverability and would have put up a good fight against the P-40 or, for that matter, even the Corsair or Hellcat. But McLeane had no intention of sending off a letter to Hirohito with his opinion. For whatever might be going on in the sky, McLeane had a front row seat, and the good guys seemed to have the upper hand.

The air war went on until well after dawn. Except for an occasional Jap patrol boat and one wild boar, frightened by the shelling on what used to be Hill 457, McLeane saw nothing. Once they'd cleared away the last annoying Japs, that part of the Huon peninsula coast made a safe haven for the Rangers and the Catalina.

Weary, his shirt torn, a carbine at the other end of his useless arm, McLeane pulled himself on board the Catalina.

The moment she saw him, a little angry, a little sad, a little relieved, his hair disheveled, Sally loved McLeane.

McLeane regarded the female passengers, especially the Gorai, without comment. In the front of the plane he found Corrigan asleep slumped over the instrument panel.

"Wake up."

McLeane shook him.

"Or do I have to kiss you and turn into a frog?"

Corrigan bolted upright in his seat, rubbed his eyes, and looked around.

"Welcome to the world, sleeping beauty."

Corrigan looked annoyed.

"What kind of contraband do we have in the back?"

Corrigan looked confused.

"The women, Corrigan. The women! You smuggling them in or out?"

"That's a long story. Let's get out of here. Is it time?"

"It's been time, friend. I was ready to go ten hours ago."

The engines started right up. The Catalina moved easily across the water and slowly into a clear, Pacific sky. McLeane took his place next to Corrigan in the copilot's seat.

"What's wrong with your arm?"

"Tennis elbow, Corrigan. Tennis elbow."

"O.K., you want to know about the ladies."

Corrigan told McLeane about the ladies, going on at great length about his part in their rescue.

"And by the way," he added. "The blond one's mine. You can have the brunette."

"Frankly, I hadn't noticed either one," McLeane said with a yawn.

Both of them had noticed McLeane however. Anna could tell at once that Sally had been stricken.

"I know," said Anna, keeping her voice low. "You think he's gorgeous."

"Don't you?"

"Yes, but he's not my type."

"I thought *men* were your type."

"They are, and stop staring at the front of the plane. You look ridiculous, and you'll get a sore neck.''

The Rangers had taken positions along the fuse-lage, except for Wilkins who lay with his foot stretched out in the middle of the plane. None of the men had much to say to the women when they came on board. They politely introduced themselves, asked no questions, and promptly fell asleep or into some relaxed state of semiconsciousness.

Periodically, for example, Contardo found his eyes open, and every time he did he found himself looking at the brunette named Anna. Now, he had seen brunettes before, even brunettes named Anna. But something about this one bothered him, and he hadn't said two real words to her.

Wilkins noticed Contardo and kicked him with his good foot. Contardo paid no attention.

''What you looking at, Contardo?'' Wilkins wore a big grin.

Contardo leaned back, his eyes closed, and an-swered Wilkins with his middle finger.

Anna did not miss the action between Contar-do and Wilkins. She smiled at Contardo's over-size nose sticking out from under his fatigue cap.

Meanwhile the Catalina headed, untroubled, to-ward Vella la Vella. Corrigan said nothing much, and McLeane went over the events of the last sev-eral hours in his mind.

Flagg had been right about half the information he had given the Rangers. He was right about the half that allowed them to do the job. He was wrong about the half that almost cost them their lives. The more McLeane thought about the latter half in the quiet blue twelve thousand miles above the ocean, the angrier he got.

"You all right?" Corrigan asked finally.

"Fine," he replied in a way that let Corrigan know he was not fine.

Suddenly, McLeane felt the presence of a figure behind him.

"Can I get you guys anything?"

The question annoyed McLeane.

"I'm Sally." She offered her hand awkwardly between the seats.

"Charmed," said McLeane flatly, extending himself to the limits of politeness.

"No, seriously, Major? Captain?"

Corrigan patted her hand.

"I'll take a double Scotch up, and give the men anything they want."

Sally returned to the back of the plane.

"Couldn't you have been a little nice to her, Mack?"

"No."

Neither Corrigan nor McLeane said much for the remainder of the flight.

General Thompson watched the Catalina land. Just a few hours before a plane carrying Margot had taken off for Darwin, Australia, a large center where the Allies took their rest and recreation. She'd gone reluctantly, only on orders. She wanted to see McLeane.

As the Catalina hit the water, McLeane wondered how long it would take him to find Flagg. He had already decided that Flagg would be first on his agenda. That pompous ass had put the Rangers through hell with misinformation. McLeane had a need to express his displeasure all over Flagg's face.

The Catalina stopped, and General Thompson waded through the water to meet the Rangers. He felt proud and relieved and just wanted to shake everyone's hand.

Even before Heinman and Contardo could ease Wilkins out of the plane, McLeane went to look for Flagg. He walked past Thompson, stopped, and turned.

"Where's Flagg?"

With McLeane, Thompson never stood on the usual military protocol. While McLeane was always respectful of rank, Thompson never insisted McLeane call him *sir* or stand when he came to mess or display the other gestures of deference due a general. Still, McLeane had never been rude until that very moment.

"Where's Flagg, damn it?"

Thompson did not like the look in McLeane's eyes. When he got no immediate answer, McLeane walked on.

All the Rangers had disembarked and were moving onto the beach together with the women. Thompson did not notice them. More important matters demanded his attention.

"Mack, where are you going?"

McLeane kept walking.

Thompson went after him on the double.

"Major, I asked you a question. I want an answer."

McLeane stopped.

"I'm going to find Major Flagg, sir, who, I imagine, is sitting on his ass in the canteen drinking coffee."

"And what do you have to say to Major Flagg, Major?" Thompson found himself trotting alongside McLeane.

"What I have to say to Flagg is personal, between him and me."

"I don't like this Mack. I've never seen you like this before."

"Well, you're seeing me like this now."

The Rangers had stopped on the shore to get their belongings together. They had a short walk across the island to their quarters.

"I've never seen the Old Man like this," Contardo commented.

"Yes, what the hell is wrong with him?" Corrigan seemed genuinely perplexed.

"He's burned. And when I say burned, I mean *burned*," Wilkins volunteered from his reclining position on the beach.

"He thinks Flagg fucked us," O'Connor said to Corrigan.

"And he did," added Heinman. "Let's face it. Normally, he'd be worrying about Wilkins here."

"Yes," said O'Connor. "Normally, he'd have a whole fucking platoon of medics down here to fuss over this worthless asshole."

Wilkins smiled. He knew affection when he heard it.

"Well, one person I don't want to be right now is Major Flagg." With that Contardo spoke for all the

Rangers.

Off to the side, the two nurses seemed a little bewildered. The three Gorai clutched each other in absolute fear.

Heinman noticed them.

"Gentlemen, we are failing in our duties as hosts."

" 'Gentlemen we are failing in our duties as hosts,' " Contardo repeated. "Why can't you talk fucking English. Just because you went to fucking Oxford or whatever the fuck they call that place . . . Over there they taught you how to talk funny, Heinie, so that nobody understands you."

Heinman understood Contardo very well. Things with the Rangers were back to normal. He had begun to worry. They hadn't really insulted each other for almost twelve hours.

"Ladies." Heinman decided to play the role. "Our accommodations are waiting. You know what it's like with the tents we use. They will require only a few minutes to clean and tidy. Meanwhile, could I interest you in the view?"

Contardo went over to Anna.

"He's really a great guy, Heinie, here. But all that ed-u-ca-tion softened his brain. In the meantime why don't you stay with me tonight?"

Anna eyeballed him.

"And where do you stay?"

"At the Vella la Vella Ritz Hilton."

Then reality hit him. He slept with a tentmate. No matter. He could get rid of him.

Anna looked at his over-large nose and wiry body. He reminded her of an Italian imp. She liked

168

him, thought he was cute.

"Don't worry," Contardo said with a wink. "The Ritz is very accommodating."

Anna smiled. Sally followed McLeane with her eyes as he disappeared over the horizon with Thompson trotting at his side.

"Mack? Where are you going, Mack?"

"I'm going to the canteen, General, sir, to find that faggot Flagg, sir."

McLeane stopped short, and looked directly at Thompson.

"And when I find him, General, sir. I'm going to kill him,"

McLeane didn't wait for a response.

"You can't do that, Mack."

Thompson ran to catch up to McLeane.

"O.K., Arch. I won't do that." He turned and looked back at the general. "I'll just put him in the hospital for a very long time."

Thompson was out of breath.

"I'll have to court-martial you, Mack." Thompson sounded very serious.

"When I'm finished with Flagg, sir, you'll have to put me in front of a firing squad."

"Mack . . ."

"I will settle for nothing less."

McLeane had fire in his eyes and murder in his heart. Thompson could only chase after him.

Major Imamura had just returned from meeting General Sasaki. He faced his commandos by the light of early morning. They had drilled and practiced and practiced and drilled. They hung on Imamura's every word.

"Our orders are very clear," he told the troops in a subdued voice. "We must destroy McLeane's Rangers."

The orders may have been clear, but the mission would not be easy, he thought to himself.

"We will move out shortly."

Imamura headed back to his tent without dismissing the men.

"When will that be, Major?" Captain Nara called after Imamura.

"That will be shortly, when you are told. By night. Everyone will be there." Imamura talked over his shoulder and then disappeared into his tent.

The commandos buzzed among themselves.

"We will be victorious," Captain Nara said prophetically.

"I shall kill each Ranger myself with these hands." Corporal Anami held up his hands.

"They shall know the cruel sting of the Japanese bullet," Sergeant Tojo volunteered.

Captain Iwabuchi swore to blow the entire island apart or face dishonor on the point of his own sword.

Private Kurito would lead the way. "I will lead you safely to their death," he said solemnly.

Sergeant Nagasaki also contributed to the demise of the Rangers. He would see that they died slowly and horribly in honor of the Emperor.

The lieutenant had doubts about all of this. He thought they had a good chance, but he never underestimated his enemy. The Rangers would fall, but they would not be easy.

Only Imamura sitting in his tent had any idea of the odds. He had the book on the Rangers and knew they could be tough. But even he had much to learn.

Fifteen

"What happened to your arm, Mack?"

They were approaching the canteen, and Thompson thought he would get McLeane's mind off Flagg.

"Tennis elbow," McLeane said bursting into the tent.

Flagg sat behind a cup of coffee, going over the papers on his clipboard, rearranging them, looking very serious. He did not see McLeane.

McLeane walked over to his table.

"Now let's see if I got it right, Flagg." McLeane's tone of voice made Flagg very nervous. "After we make this ridiculous drop on Hill 457 —did I get the number right, Flagg?—only a few sentries will be there and we should take them out with no trouble. Just one little machine gun. We won't mention the other patrol that got in our way up there.

"Now we drop the bomb and call for artillery which comes, God bless them. We've got artillery all over the place. And we go down the north side just as you said, Flagg. It's nice and easy, a piece of cake. All the Japs are over on the north side worried about MacArthur.

"It makes a lovely movie, Flagg, only that isn't what happened."

McLeane banged the table with his good arm.

"There were Japs on the north side of the mountain, too, Flagg, *all over* the north side of the mountain, and they were on us as soon as we dropped the bomb. We damn near got blown up.

"And there were Japs on the coast when we got there and a whole goddamn air war going on. We had to sit, Flagg, sit and wait for more Japs who weren't supposed to be there to make Swiss cheese out of us."

Thompson stood anxiously a few feet behind McLeane.

"Did you clear all this intelligence with the Japs before you sent us out there? Did you ask if it would be all right with them?"

Suddenly, McLeane kicked the table over.

"I'm talking to you, goddamn it!"

Flagg had jumped out of the way and stood in front of his fallen chair absolutely terrified.

"We do the best we—"

Flagg had no time to get the sentence out. McLeane was on him. They both went down.

Thompson called for the MPs.

In no time McLeane had Flagg pinned at the

174

shoulders with his knees. He smashed his face repeatedly with a succession of rights.

In one frantic burst, Flagg kicked McLeane off. McLeane fell backward against the table. He hit his head in a way that stunned him for a split second. When he opened his eyes, Flagg had drawn his automatic. He stood above McLeane huffing, his face battered, twisted.

"Flagg!" Thompson screamed from the sidelines.

Flagg just looked down at McLeane.

"Don't do this McLeane. We do the best we can in intelligence."

He kept moving around McLeane.

"Sometimes we make mistakes. Not often, but we do make them."

"Flag! McLeane!"

Thompson could only yell. Neither man paid attention to him. They had their own score to settle. A few other troops had gathered around, but far outside the ring.

Suddenly, McLeane's legs shot out and trapped Flagg's ankles in a scissors. Flagg tripped. The automatic inadvertently went off putting a hole in the canteen tent. Flagg stumbled and dropped the gun. McLeane dove and got to it two seconds before Flagg.

By that time the Rangers had heard about the goings on in the canteen and had run to help out McLeane. They stopped dead as soon as they saw General Thompson. At that moment, Thompson could have committed murder with a stare. Anyway, they decided, McLeane didn't need help.

McLeane had Flagg down again and was pistol-whipping him with Flagg's own automatic. Sally, who, along with Anna, had joined the Rangers, turned her head. Each time the butt of the automatic hit Flagg's head he let out a groan.

"I can't watch this," Sally said, and Anna took her out of the tent.

"This is how we play war out there, Flagg." McLeane had lost his head. "This is what we do with your intelligence."

Anna stuck her head inside and whispered to Contardo. "MPs are coming."

"Quick," he said to the other Rangers. In a flash they were on top of both majors.

Thompson wanted to say something, but he wanted the fight stopped more than anything, and the Rangers had stopped the fight.

O'Connor dragged Flagg away. He was unconscious and, O'Connor feared, hurt badly. He then went over to help Contardo and Heinman with McLeane.

"I'm not finished, goddamn it! I want him. I just want him!"

"Hold him," Contardo said to O'Connor and Heinman.

"We're trying," Heinman yelled.

"Someday, not right away, but someday, you're going to thank me for this, Major." With that, Contardo hit McLeane so hard with a right uppercut that he fell over and the other three fell down.

Just then the MPs walked in the tent.

"You called us, sir," a sergeant asked General Thompson. Thompson, shaken by what he had just seen, did not answer right away.

"There's no problem here, Sergeant," said Heinman getting up. "Everything has been taken care of."

"Well, the general here gave us a call." The sergeant could see McLeane out cold and, opposite him, Flagg, whose face looked like a dish of dog food. He could also see the turned-over tables and the hole in the tent.

Finally, Thompson got his voice back.

"I did call you, Sergeant," he said. "I want those two men arrested."

He pointed to Flagg and McLeane. He spoke with great effort. Clearly, he did not want to arrest either one, but Marine regulations gave him no choice.

Then, as though they had been choreographed, O'Connor and Contardo stood in front of McLeane, and Heinman blocked the MPs' way.

"With all due respect, General, Sergeant, no one is taking the major. We will take care of him. Meanwhile, I suggest someone look after Major Flagg. He looks very badly hurt."

"I have my orders, sir."

The MP sergeant seemed perplexed.

"I'm sure you do, Sergeant, and I really don't want to make your job difficult. But we take care of our own. We have had a rough day, you could say, and we would very much like to take a shower. I promise you, however, that if you want Major McLeane, you will have to go through me to get him. And if you get through me—which I doubt—I know you won't get through them."

He pointed to Contardo and O'Connor who, just standing there, made a very convincing argument.

"Is this insubordination, Lieutenant?" General Thompson already seemed tired of the whole business.

"Call it want you want to, sir. I'm explaining reality as clearly as I can."

General Thompson turned to the MP sergeant.

"Thank you, Sergeant, but forget it."

The MPs left the tent without comment.

"Take McLeane to his quarters, Lieutenant, and get a medic over here on the double."

Thompson went over to the unconscious body of Flagg.

Contardo smiled as he slung McLeane's frame across his shoulder. How many times had he saved the Rangers from the MPs? Now they had a chance to return the favor.

O'Connor helped Wilkins hobble in the sand.

"I bet the Old Man kicked that faggot's ass into next week." Wilkins didn't get to see the action.

"Let's just call it an early knockout."

The Rangers at that moment looked like a parade of the walking dead.

Wilkins was laid up with a compound fracture. McLeane's left supraspinatus muscle had been badly ripped. Flagg did not have brain damage.

They all refused to be flown to a hospital.

"I don't give a good rat's ass what happens to my leg," Wilkins insisted. "Ain't nobody moving me no place."

Just to make sure the powers that be got the message, Wilkins catnapped with a loaded Smith & Wesson across his lap.

McLeane sat up in his own bed and glowered every time Thompson suggested he be shipped out to Australia for treatment.

Flagg, when he finally gained consciousness, signed a formal document absolving the Rangers of all responsibility for his injuries. He was a wimp but no dummy.

General Archibald Thompson shuttled among the three of them with a worried look on his face.

Fortunately, Colonel Percival Entwhistle, a top surgeon with the Australian Royal Navy happened to be in the area, and General Thompson was able to enlist his services. Setting Wilkins' leg went without complication.

"Pretty routine, this," the colonel mumbled. "Possible infection." He was covered with plaster.

Colonel Entwhistle, a man of little talk, spoke in lumps of words rather than in anything like sentences.

He gave Wilkins a tetanus shot large enough to cure hoof-and-mouth disease in a whole herd of cows. It hurt like hell, and Wilkins did not make a sound, but his eyes watered a lot.

McLeane, especially cranky, wanted no part of any doctor.

"Just leave the damn thing alone. It'll take care of itself."

Entwhistle knocked McLeane out with an injection. Then, assisted by Sally and Anna, he stitched the muscle and sewed up the outer wound.

"Should hurt a lot when he wakes up," Entwhistle commented. "Give him these."

He left a small bottle of pain killer with the two nurses.

Flagg proved to be more interesting as a case. McLeane had damaged his face rather than his cranium. All thought processes remained in tact. No nerves had been damaged. His nose and jaw were both broken. Nothing could be done with the nose. Entwhistle did, however, wire Flagg's jaw, and the jaw would have to stay wired for six to eight weeks. Meanwhile, Flagg had to live with a sore, swollen face.

When McLeane heard the news he felt relieved that permanent damage had happened to Flagg and he was amused that Flagg would have to drink his meals through a straw for the next two months and, most of all, that Flagg would be unable to say anything.

"This is not funny, Mack," General Thompson assured him as he tried to keep from laughing.

"Laughing makes me hurt," said McLeane, coughing.

"I could have you both up on charges. I could have you both in jail. I could—"

"I'm sorry, General, I truly am." McLeane sounded almost sincere. "But the man is dangerous. He's self-important and—"

"Major!" General Thompson cut him short. "The discussion is ended. I never want to see a demonstration like that again. It could cost you your career."

Both men were silent for a moment.

"But I'm not pressing anything, Mack. Frankly,

180

you're too good, and I need you too much."

After a few moments of silence, General Thompson started to chuckle.

"Poor Flagg. He looks so awful, and he hurts so much."

McLeane broke up with laughter.

"It isn't right to laugh, and I'm sort of sorry for taking him apart, but the thought of him with his jaw wired and a pair of glasses perched on his nose which is now all over his face breaks me up. Let's hear him say 'according to intelligence sources' now."

McLeane's laughing caused his shoulder to hurt and the doctor had said he should avoid any excitement. When she heard him making noise, Sally ran to his bed with the painkiller.

"Major," she said very professionally. "I think you should take two of these right now."

McLeane took the bottle of pills and flung them across the room; then he grasped his left shoulder and doubled over, still laughing, but clearly in pain.

Colonel Entwhistle had left the island. If anything happened medically, McLeane would be in trouble.

"Mack, take it easy, Mack."

General Thompson could not afford to have McLeane take a turn for the worse. He needed him with a good left shoulder.

McLeane stopped laughing and coughing. His shoulder hurt more than ever, but he didn't let them know that. Finally, he just lay back on the many pillows Sally had scrounged for him and tried not to think of Flagg's broken jaw.

"I'm leaving you in this good lady's capable hands, Mack," Thompson said, when McLeane had settled down. "I don't want any reports about your not following doctor's orders."

McLeane had closed his eyes.

"Take care of him," Thompson said to Sally. "And if he gives you any problems, call me at once."

On his way out of McLeane's quarters, Thompson turned. "Did you hear me, Mack?"

McLeane winked and gave him a thumbs-up sign.

General Thompson disappeared shaking his head.

Sally stood by the man in bed, already desperately in love with him, glad to be there, unsure of what would happen next.

Sixteen

Anna Pucci divided her time between caring for Private Wilkins and Major Flagg. After a week of convalescence, Flagg looked almost recognizable. The swelling had gone down. He could open his eyes. His nose had been so badly broken, however, that his glasses continually slipped off what used to be the bridge. That caused him a certain frustration. Otherwise, he felt no pain, and began, early on, to reorganize the papers on his clipboard.

As for Wilkins, his leg did not look good. Suspecting that the infection had not gone away, Anna, with Sally's help, removed Colonel Entwhistle's expertly made cast to find a large inflamed area between the ankle and the knee.

"Doesn't this hurt, Wilkins?" Anna asked in disbelief.

Wilkins, who answered all questions holding his

Smith & Wesson, shook his head in the negative.

"Well, we're going to leave this exposed." Anna did not believe him.

The two women fashioned a kind of strap on poles coming up from the floor. On this Wilkins could hang his leg. Given conditions on Vella la Vella, they managed to make a pretty decent traction sling.

Once in it, Wilkins realized that he would have even less mobility than he did in the cast.

"What the hell's going on here?"

People heard him yelling halfway across the island.

"Why are you bothering with me at all?" he screamed at Anna. "I can damn well take care of myself. Why don't you tie up old Contardo over there the way you done me? He'd love to have you tie him up. Then he could tie you up. You two could have a good old time instead of you fooling around with me. I don't need it."

In fact, Anna had long had her eye on Contardo. Working as she did with Wilkins, who was sleeping in the same tent with Contardo, she could hardly not have her eye on him. She liked what she saw.

No one ever called Contardo handsome. The size of his nose alone made him ineligible for that category. Anyway, he would not have appreciated being called handsome. He preferred to think of himself as animal, and Anna felt a lot of unleashed panther in him. He always seemed coiled, ready to spring. Even relaxed on his cot or after mess, he seemed ready to explode. He had a small, tight body and a fast mouth. He made her laugh. Along with everything else, she thought of him as a funny little man.

Contardo also had his eye on Anna, and he, too, liked what he saw. He liked her dark hair and eyes, full mouth and body. He liked the way she took over situations, cared for Wilkins. He liked tough broads and Anna was tough.

Anna and Contardo had many opportunities to look at each other. After all, she spent a great deal of every day where he and the Rangers lived and slept. It was only a matter of time before they would spend long hours alone. The first time came after Anna had spent an especially hard hour with Wilkins, trying to get him to keep still.

Heinman had gone for a walk. O'Connor sat in front of his tent drawing plans for ways to improve the bomb he had made. Contardo lay in bed with his right leg crossed over his left, lost in the pretense of thought. Actually, the way Anna's breasts hung down in her dress when she bent over Wilkins' leg was driving Contardo slowly mad.

"Forget that ignorant hillbilly," he said to Anna suddenly. "He doesn't appreciate what you do for him anyway."

"Yeah," Wilkins chimed in. "Forget me. I'm an ignorant hillbilly who don't appreciate nothing."

"Come on," said Contardo springing off the bed. "I'll take you to dinner. We'll have drinks, go dancing. I think Harry James is playing tonight."

"Where're you going dancing around here?" Wilkins asked.

"See how ignorant he is?"

Contardo grabbed Anna and, imitating a trumpet,

danced her around Wilkins.

"Is that some kind of song we're supposed to be dancing to?" Anna was amused.

"That is 'I'm in the Mood for Love.' "

"You should hear him sing," Wilkins volunteered. "He's the only guinea in the world who can't carry a tune."

Contardo held Anna at a polite distance. He moved gracefully, she noticed.

"Do you like to dance?" she asked coyly.

"Dancing's okay."

Wilkins looked up.

"Ever since I've known him," he said, "I've heard about how bad he was and how he used to beat up cops and steal from crooks. None of that's true. He was a lover boy. He spent all his time dancing."

Contardo kept right on making sounds like a trumpet and right on dancing with Anna. He danced her out the entrance of the tent and onto the sand.

"Lover boy!" Wilkins shouted after him.

"Eat your heart out!" Contardo called back.

They could not dance on sand. Contardo let go of Anna.

"You do dance very well," she said.

"Thanks. I'll never hear the end of it from him." He pointed back to the tent.

A warm fall evening began to settle in over Vella la Vella. The skies were clear of planes. The hint of a breeze came off the ocean. The world had suddenly gone silent. They stood and looked at each other for a while.

"I don't deal with silence too good," Contardo

said awkwardly. "I like noise. I'm Italian."

"Me, too. Anna Pucci."

Contardo brightened.

"Hey. Isn't that a coincidence?"

"Yes."

Anna enjoyed Contardo's discomfort. In fact, she had to work hard to keep from laughing out loud.

"Well, Anna Pucci, the night is young, and I have a Class A pass in my pocket. Can I interest you in dinner on the terrace overlooking France or would you prefer a cruise on my yacht around the Greek islands."

He hesitated a moment.

"They do have islands around Greece don't they? I mean, I did say it right?"

This time Anna *did* laugh.

"Yes, they have islands around Greece."

"That's good," he said with relief. "I don't know too much about that stuff."

"Let's get a cup of coffee while I make up my mind."

They headed toward the canteen.

"You from Brooklyn?" he asked.

"No, but you are."

"Yes, how'd you know?"

"Military intelligence."

"That I don't want to hear. Come on, where're you from?"

"Philadelphia."

He stopped.

"Philly. South Philly."

"Yes. Do you know Philadelphia?"

"A little. I got an aunt down there around Sixteenth and Jackson.''

"I'm from further down. Second and Wolf.''

He approached the next question with caution.

"I bet you root for the Phillies.''

"Suppose I do?''

"They stink. That's all.''

"Well I happen to like them.''

For the first time since talking with Anna, Contardo felt comfortable. He loved fighting only slightly more than baseball, and he knew more about baseball than anyone alive.

"Look, Anna, you don't have to like a team because you come from their town. That's ridiculous.''

Anna said nothing. Contardo couldn't shut up.

"They've been in the basement of the national league for the last three years in a row. And the year before that they were next to last. They have the worst infield in baseball—Etten, Glossop, May, and Bragen.''

If Contardo expected Anna to be impressed with his command of baseball facts, he was disappointed.

"What's all this about anyway?'' she asked. "I root for the Phillies. My father roots for the Phillies. So do my brothers and my uncles and my cousins. I'm from Philadelphia.''

"But they're the worst team in the history of the game.''

Anna found herself getting slightly annoyed, as though someone were insulting her and for no reason. Meanwhile, Contardo, engrossed in his favorite subject, became more intense.

"Now the Dodgers, the Dodgers are a team."

His face lit up.

"They've got Reiser in center, Reese at short, Wyatt and and Higbe pitching. And do you know what they've got? Do you know?"

"No, what have they got?"

Contardo missed the irritation in her voice.

"They've got the best manager in the history of any sport. That's what they've got."

He stopped to emphasize his point.

"They've got Leo Durocher."

He spoke the name slowly, clearly, almost reverentially.

"Do they have Leo Durocher?" Anna asked mimicking Contardo's voice.

"Yes, of course."

Contardo seemed perplexed.

"Then I think you should take him on a cruise of the Greek islands tonight," Anna informed him and stormed off, sand flying behind her.

Contardo stood and watched her go, sure he had done something wrong, but not sure just what.

McLeane had been up and out of bed for a couple of days and could even take short walks around the island before the pain in his shoulder got to him and Sally sat him down.

"You have a terrible wound," she reassured him without being sure how to address him. After a week, McLeane sensed her difficulty.

"Just call me, Mack."

But she didn't really feel quite comfortable with that.

"You have a terrible wound . . . Mack. And I expect your arm to be in a sling for another five weeks."

"It better not be."

"Well, Colonel Entwhistle should be coming through about then, and he said he would make a determination . . ."

"It's my shoulder. I make determinations about my shoulder."

"Yes, Major . . . I mean, Mack."

Sally had fallen so deeply in love with Mack that even he could see it. She spent every waking minute with him and even watched him sleep. Even the most badly torn supraspinatus muscle did not warrant such care. She fawned over him and mooned after him. On the one hand that kind of attention annoyed him. On the other hand he had noticed the way her breasts jiggled under her white uniform and how the uniform rode up her thigh when she crossed her legs.

"I'm hungry," he said. "Is it time for dinner yet?"

"They've been serving for a while. Shall I bring you dinner?"

He didn't want her to bring him dinner. He wanted to go to the mess and eat among men. But from the look on her face he would probably disappoint her if he didn't let her get it, so he said yes. And she seemed so excited when she brought back both meals on a tray.

Creamed beef on toast has always been creamed beef on toast, and McLeane did his best to eat it. As Sally reminded him, however, it *was* hot, and she had been able to get them each an extra piece of chocolate cake.

She watched him eat.

"Is it all right?"

Why did she want to know? Had she cooked it?

"Aren't you eating?" he asked.

"Yes."

She seemed even more nervous than usual and avoided his eyes. McLeane felt something coming, but nothing came. They ate in silence.

She did look awfully good, he thought to himself. Uniform white suited her. A lock of blonde hair had fallen onto her forehead. She had put on lipstick and, sitting opposite him, had crossed her legs.

Corrigan also thought Sally looked awfully good, but he never got to see her much since returning to Vella la Vella from the raid on the Huon Peninsula. For one thing, he had decided to make himself scarce after McLeane and Flagg got into it, and for another thing, Sally seemed to prefer the company of McLeane, and for still another thing, he wanted the time to do maintenance on the Catalina. In other words, Corrigan kept a low profile.

He had seen Sally off and on, mostly at the canteen or mess hall. At such times he always asked about McLeane.

"He's doing very well," Sally always answered.

Of course, Corrigan did not really care. He knew, however, that Sally did, and he also knew that, otherwise, she did not especially want to talk to him.

On the very evening that Sally managed to secure two extra pieces of chocolate cake, Corrigan walked her back to McLeane's quarters. Seeing her again and standing close to her fired his lust, and he decided to make one final direct assault on his target.

"Look, Sally," he said just before she brought McLeane his dinner, "come up in the Catalina with me. I'll show you the war from the air."

"Thank you, Captain," she said politely, "but I'm busy for the evening."

"McLeane?"

Sally nodded her head.

Even though he knew it well enough, Corrigan did not like to have the fact confirmed for him, and he did not like finding himself in such a defensive position. Standing in front of a woman like a schoolboy in heat hardly enhanced his image of himself.

"What is it Sally?" His voice snapped with anger.

She did not say anything.

"I mean, is he *so* terrific?"

He saw the answer all over her face.

"I'll see you around," he said finally and went off in a huff. McLeane had never been his favorite person anyway. Maybe he had difficulty liking him because of professional jealousy. Sally's choice of McLeane over himself only added insult to further insult. He kicked the sand on his way back to the Catalina.

He came upon the Catalina floating freely in the water and stopped to really look at her. She really looked fine. With all her parts still intact no seaplane looked better.

For an instant a vision flashed through his mind

192

of Sally as she bent slightly to enter McLeane's tent with a tray of too much food. The white uniform clung to her hips and molded her perfect buttocks.

Well, at least he could depend on the Catalina. So far she had made it through the war in good shape.

Seventeen

". . . because you got no style with the ladies, Contardo."

Contardo lay on his bunk listening to Wilkins lecture on women. Anna had just come to tend Wilkins' bad leg and had gone. She spoke to everyone except Contardo.

"He's right," added O'Connor, who still worked diligently on plans for the perfect bomb. "You don't understand. You gotta woo them."

"What?"

"You got to woo them."

Contardo did not know what that meant and did not want to display his ignorance by asking.

"It means you've got to coax them sweetly," Heinman volunteered, looking up from his latest issue of *Studies in Oriental Anthropology*.

"Yeah," Wilkins continued. "She don't care

about baseball. What are you doing telling her about baseball?''

"I care about baseball.''

Contardo sat bolt upright.

"Yes, baseball and killing Japs.'' O'Connor enjoyed this. "You are some lover, Contardo.''

Contardo felt not only rejected by Anna but also foolish in front of his comrades.

"You have got to be sweet. That is the word we are looking for, 'sweet.' '' Heinman stated.

The idea of a sweet Contardo cracked them all up.

"Now how can we make Contardo sweet?'' Wilkins hadn't had so much fun since the Rangers were on Lonelyville and Contardo went up for his first jump from the tower.

"Now he dances sweet.'' Wilkins tried to be positive.

"Yeah, but where're you gonna dance around here?'' O'Connor followed the truth wherever it led.

They all gave the matter more thought before Wilkins began again on an up note.

"Maybe if you just don't say nothin' . . . Let's face it Contardo. It's your mouth that gets you in trouble. Of course, you ain't much to look at with that nose. But the ladies can see that as well as anybody and it don't seem to put them off.

"You are a true war hero. I give you that. I could say a lot of rotten things about you, but one thing I have seen with my eyes is the way you kill Japs, and on killing Japs and fighting generally you are the best. Now, a lady has got to love that.

"She don't have to mind your nose, and you are a true hero. You got money on you. I know you don't make much, but you don't spend nothing either and, Christ, man, we're on a desert island. You have got to be better than Clark Gable. At least you're here.

"No, it seems to me that the problem lies with your mouth. You open it and the ladies go away."

"How much would it hurt if I came over and jumped on your leg, Wilkins? The bad one, the one in the sling."

"Now that ain't sweet. You see what I mean?"

Contardo got up and went outside where a late morning rain had started to fall in slow drops, far apart. He never said a word. The world seemed bright, all sand beige and blue. No one would ever know this was a war zone.

He didn't understand the word *woo,* and he didn't understand the word *sweet* either, he guessed. In Flatbush such matters were handled more directly, more simply. All he ever had to do was snap his fingers and point. There the women came from out of trees to do what he wanted. But that was in Flatbush. Evidently, the rules were different on Vella la Vella.

The morning once again found Sally hovering over McLeane. The signs of rain and then the rain itself curtailed his activity outside. McLeane, with Sally looking at him all the time, went stir crazy very easily. First he wanted to read, then he wanted to sleep, but a pair of deep blue eyes would not let go of him.

McLeane had always tried to be a nice guy, but

sometimes even his greatest efforts failed. He took Sally in his sights. A sweeter, lusher lady he might never see again. The way her whole body jiggled as she straightened up the mess he'd made from being confined to quarters, the way her breasts bounced as she made the bunk led him to believe that he ought to take direct action.

"Sally," he said finally, "we have a problem. You are making me nuts, driving me out of my mind . . . so to speak."

He got up from the bunk where she had propped him up on pillows scrounged by the supply sergeant. She turned quickly.

"Yes?"

At that moment the voice of Gen. Archibald Thompson could be heard through the tent.

"Mack? Mack!"

General Thompson seldom entered McLeane's tent without an invitation. This time he seemed greatly exercised. He went straight ahead, his swagger stick preceding him.

"Mack, this can't go on."

McLeane had no idea what Thompson meant.

"This is the third call and it can't go on. Margot has radioed . . . ."

He noticed Sally and stopped.

"Sorry, Mack."

He headed to leave.

"What's the problem, sir?"

McLeane followed him with his arm in a sling.

"She keeps calling here. She's using an open frequency. I can't have it! That's all. I can't have it!"

General Thompson disappeared waving his arms

in an uncharacteristic show of frustration.

"Sir!" McLeane called the General back and gestured with his right arm. The move hurt the whole left side of his back and caused him to cry out. He plopped down hard on his bunk.

He had had it. Margot needed a rest and so did he. She belonged in Australia. He knew she wanted to find out how the mission went, how he felt, if he had been hurt. But with all her experience at a radio she should have known better. Signals between Darwin and Vella la Vella would be so easy for the enemy to pick up. Thompson had every right to be angry.

He looked up at Sally.

"I need some time alone," he said; then he noticed the hurt expression on her face.

"I appreciate everything you've done, Sally, I really do. But the two of us together in these small quarters all the time isn't working. I am perfectly capable of taking care of myself."

The more he said, the worse he made matters. She started to go. She did have a lovely butt, he thought.

"Who's Margot?" Sally asked, before leaving.

"A friend," McLeane answered.

"Does she live here?"

"Sometimes."

"I shouldn't have asked."

She left, and McLeane felt he had done an awful but necessary thing. He relaxed for the first time in days.

* * *

199

By nightfall Contardo had taken action. After mess, he combed the island. Anna had just left Flagg. Contardo found her walking the beach alone. She seemed at least as unhappy as he about the turn their relationship had taken.

"Anna! Anna Pucci!" he called after her. She did not stop, but he caught up with her anyway.

"Look," he said out of breath and grabbing her arm. "You're gonna listen to me."

"What?"

She folded her arms and turned her head away.

"I want you to be my woman."

Anna laughed out loud.

"Hey, you laughing at me? Don't ever laugh at me."

He pulled her to him, held her tight at the waist, kissed her full on the mouth and felt her body relax in his arms.

"Don't ever laugh at me," he said again in a firm, but hoarse voice. "Did you hear what I said?"

She nodded.

"Well, then say something, damn it! When I ask a question, give me an answer . . . with your mouth."

"I'm not laughing at you."

She could not look at him and her voice trembled slightly. He ran his hands down her body and over her breasts. She could feel his hardness. He kissed her again.

"My woman," he whispered in her ear.

They clung together in the light of the half-moon which hung over Vella la Vella. She kissed his chest, between the first two open buttons of his fatigue shirt and moved up higher with her tongue along his neck. She pulled his head down to her and nibbled on his ear.

This is right, Contardo thought. This is how life should be between man and woman. He let Anna enjoy herself, honor his perfect body. Then he felt her breath in his ear.

Suddenly a sharp pain went through his head. Contardo grabbed his ear.

"You bit me. You fucking bit me."

He could not believe what happened. Anna raced, laughing, down the beach.

"I'll get you, you bitch."

Contardo took off after her. She was laughing too hard to run well. After several yards, Contardo dived, tripped her, and pinned her in the sand. She put up a good struggle to get away, but Contardo held her in a steely grip.

He had her where he wanted her.

After a while she stopped struggling. She looked up at him, trying to catch her breath, trying not to laugh.

"That's funny, huh? Biting my fucking ear is funny?"

"Yes." She started laughing all over again.

Contardo watched her chest heave. He smiled down at her wickedly.

"Funny, huh? Very funny."

Slowly, deftly he unbottoned the first button of her dress. She tried to move, but couldn't.

"Oh, no, please!"

"Very funny. You bite my ear. Funny."

He unbuttoned the second button and his smile

grew the full width of his face.

"Please, this isn't fair."

"You're right. This isn't fair. What is fair is biting my ear. Fair and funny."

He reached down and pinched her nipples, not hard, but enough to let her know that he was being fair, fair and funny.

"You're not going to do this, are you?" Contardo did not hear panic in her voice.

"Do what? What am I going to do?" He undid the third button and tickled her cleavage.

She did not answer.

He hadn't had this much fun since the tenth grade at Bay Ridge High when he took Elvira Favazza's bra and panties away behind the subway terminal on New Utrecht Avenue because she refused to suck him off during lunch. She had to go directly to cheerleader practice after school. Contardo just happened to be there with six of his friends.

On second thought, Contardo considered this evening more fun and certainly more fair than anything he had ever done with Elvira Favazza or her underwear.

He reached down and kissed her.

"I'm gonna ruin you forever, Anna," he said right in her face. "After me, you won't want anyone else."

In the background they both heard the faint strains of someone singing "Waltzing Matilda." Contardo thought he recognized the voice. Anna knew it was Corrigan.

Rather than struggle at all Anna just gave up. Contardo loosened her fourth button, and moved his hand over her breasts, which were harnessed by a bra.

She reached up to kiss him.

"Let's get rid of this." In one swift and expert move he reached behind her back and with one hand sprung her bra. His other hand found her bare flesh, and he heard her sigh.

In a moment her breasts felt the rush of evening air and Contardo was kissing her all over.

"And let's get rid of these." He reached under her as she eased up her hips and he removed her panties.

He had totally mastered her. She submitted gladly. She did not mind when her dress came off and she lay completely naked in the sand under his body. Nothing that exciting had ever happened to her.

Contardo entered her roughly and rode her without mercy, and she loved every minute, held him tight, and murmured how much she wanted him.

After Thompson stormed out of McLeane's quarters and Sally left, hurt, the major spent the best day in weeks. With no one there to watch him every second he could do what he wanted. What he wanted to do included walking around the island, visiting the Rangers, reading, sleeping, and nothing. He did them happily and well.

He thought occasionally about Margot, wondered how she might be getting along. Her sending him a direct radio message on Vella la Vella violated not only military security but also good sense. He could not believe that she had done something that stupid and hoped she was all right. He also hoped Thompson would forget about it soon.

He thought about Sally only once. She had been very sweet to him. He certainly did not want to hurt her feelings, but he looked forward to the night alone.

He was to be disappointed.

Just as McLeane was about to leave for evening mess. Sally came into his tent carrying two dinner trays.

"You've had your day alone and you probably made yourself too tired. I brought you something to eat."

She sounded overly cheerful and a little nervous as she propped pillows up around McLeane's bunk and pushed him back onto them.

"Now make yourself comfortable."

He moved like a man resigned, swung his feet up, relaxed. Sally untied his shoes.

"I want you to be quiet. I'll leave if you want . . . if I bother you."

McLeane gestured for her to sit down. He would lose, but only this time.

They ate in silence, interrupted occasionally by Sally's comments on the food, the weather, and the war. She also tried to engage McLeane in conversation, but he answered all her questions in the fewest possible words.

"Did you have a good day?"

"All right."

"What did you do?"

"Not much."

When he had finished eating, she removed his

dinner tray with unwarranted good cheer and moved over to the bed.

Neither she nor Anna had been able to procure clothes that fit, so they both continued to wear their same white uniforms which, with every washing, grew slightly tighter.

She stepped outside the tent only to return in a moment. She looked quite professional.

"May I see your arm?"

She took his arm and moved it around.

"Does this hurt? This?"

Whatever may have hurt, McLeane was not about to tell her.

When she finished her brief examination, she sat calmly on the bed and looked McLeane straight in the eye. He felt something coming that had nothing directly to do with a torn supraspinatus muscle.

"I really don't care about Margot whatever-her-name-is, Major." As she talked Sally undid the buttons on her dress. "I really don't care what kind of relationship you and she have or had or what kind of relationship you and she have when she gets back. I don't *if* she gets back."

She had completely opened the top of her uniform and undone her bra. Sally, everybody's girl next door, had turned into pure sex.

"I just want you," she said. "And I don't care about anything else."

She had pushed her dress down over her shoulders and was cupping her breasts. They were even larger than McLeane had thought and stuck straight out.

She reached over and kissed him hard; then she

pulled his face to her chest.

"I do the kissing around here," McLeane said, and he grabbed her and yanked her across his body onto the other side of the bed.

He ignored the sudden sharp pain in his shoulder.

She helped him remove the rest of her dress with his one free hand. In an instant she lay naked beside him, groaning, grinding into the bed.

"Take me, Mack. Take me," she whispered urgently.

Before he had a chance to move she climbed on him and tore at his fatigue shirt.

"Oh, easy, easy."

"I have to have you, now!"

Working with only one arm, slowed him down. Sally couldn't wait. She undressed him in record time, throwing his clothes behind her, muttering all the time how much she loved him, how strong and brave he was, how she had to have him or die.

Finally she threw herself on top of him and had an orgasm the moment he entered her soft, wet flesh.

"Oh, God! Oh, God! Oh my God!"

She bounced on him frantically, throwing her breasts in his face. She had lost all control, forgotten herself and McLeane's bad shoulder, and just exploded more times than she could count.

Sally lay on him and tossed her blond head from side to side and gasped and told him how much she loved him, told him all the things she wanted him to do to her.

"Oh, you're so good! Oh, you're so good."

McLeane grabbed her firm butt, round like marble, and pulled her to him.

"Oh you're big! Big!"

The sweet shy thing, his nurse for a week had become a tiger.

Sally began to move harder and faster. Her mutterings became less intelligible until she exploded into one ecstatic scream and collapsed on McLeane's chest.

He finished his own business quietly. The two of them lay together and said nothing for a long while.

"I love you," she said softly.

McLeane put his arm around her shoulder. He envisioned a long night.

Eighteen

Vella la Vella lay in Allied-occupied territory and was an installation of considerable importance. True, larger islands abounded in the Solomons, housing more troops and supplies. Even with Flagg there Vella la Vella hardly buzzed as a center of intelligence-gathering activity. But the island was an important base for air strikes against Japanese troops, bases, and ship convoys. The Marines billeted the Rangers on that island because it was close to the front and, Flagg assured everyone, was secure from sneak attacks by the enemy.

Nevertheless, the Rangers lived there with great caution. If O'Connor, Contardo, Heinman, and Wilkins all chose to live pretty much together, McLeane pitched his tent a bit farther away so he could entertain in privacy. Corrigan had his private lagoon apart from the others and the base's central radio control had situated itself still farther from anybody. General Thompson and Major Flagg had separate quarters elsewhere on the island. Everything on Vella la Vella was spread out except for that tiny cluster of Rangers just down the path from McLeane. That should have made everything harder to find . . . and everyone. It didn't.

That night, a week and a day after the mission on Hill 457, seconds before midnight, Major Imamura's commandos hit Vella la Vella. They had no trouble locating Vella la Vella at night or getting through the Allied defenses that missed one small rubber raft slipping onto an isolated beach.

The attack came quietly.

Contardo and Anna lay naked in the sand. They had not stopped groaning for the past four hours. He sucked gently on her breasts while she pulled his cock.

Intermittently, Corrigan sang the same verse of "Waltzing Matilda." He sounded drunk.

The Japs hit the beach, then opened fire.

Contardo dove for his automatic which lay beside his discarded pants.

"Fuck."

He wanted a machine gun.

He pulled on his boots. Quietly, quickly, he got dressed. Anna threw on her uniform over her naked body.

Suddenly they heard a loud wail.

"AAAAHHHHHHEEEEEE!"

Contardo kissed Anna softly on the lips and moved like a cat in the direction of the sound.

"I'll kill every one of you Jap cocksuckers."

210

A frantic spray of machine-gun fire followed the sound of Corrigan's voice. Contardo could tell that he had the Owen out and was using it like a crazy man.

"Kill you! Do you hear me? Kill . . ."

Corrigan was laying down bullets all over the Pacific, firing at every shadow.

Contardo came to a clearing in front of the Catalina. The plane tipped about 20 degrees to his right. The Japs had hit it. Contardo looked closer. He figured that the support between the pontoon and the wing was shot up.

Meanwhile, Corrigan had jumped from the plane and stood up to his waist in water, his machine gun rattling nonstop.

Contardo saw no one else.

Then, up the beach, he caught a glimpse of a shadow.

"Anna." Her name fell from his lips.

He bolted to where, only minutes before, they had made love together. Her white uniform could be easily spotted. Corrigan kept the fire power up and the screaming. Rather than move slowly along the beach under cover, Contardo ran. A Jap carbine opened up, and he could feel the shells pepper the sand in front of him. He dived behind the fallen trunk of a dendiki tree.

He caught his breath and tried to figure out how to get behind the Japs. He did not know how many there were much less where they were. He really wanted to use his knife, but first he would have to find someone to stick. And he wondered what had happened to Anna.

The thought of her no sooner crossed his mind than she appeared crawling around the other end of the log. He frightened her. Then she realized who it was.

"There's at least three of them," she said in a calm, low voice.

He had an idea.

"When I give you a signal, fire this."

He handed her the automatic, lay flat on the ground, and stuck his head around the log. He raised his arm and she let go with a volley.

The Japs returned fire.

He crawled back to Anna.

"Well, I know there are two of them. I have a pretty good idea where they are and some idea of where they ought to be going."

Corrigan continued to fire away a few hundred feet behind them. He wasn't hitting much, but he was keeping heads low.

"I think there's another one." Anna seemed almost certain.

"If there is, I'll meet him sooner or later."

He decided to go up and around behind the Japs. That would take longer and put him directly in their line of fire, but he wanted the cover.

He had his knife out. The adrenaline started pumping.

"Get ready," he told Anna.

"You love this don't you?"

"Not as much as I love you."

Anna knew a lie when she heard it, but she smiled.

"O.K. Give them a few rounds straight ahead."

Anna fired. The Japs reciprocated. Contardo got a bead on where they were.

"Just keep them busy once in a while," he said.

Contardo glanced behind him to see Anna, a few feet away, hunched, her behind up, the fabric straining against it.

"See you around," he said and slipped off.

McLeane saw the attack a split second before he heard it. Suddenly, bullets tore his tent in half, sailing a hair's breath from his head. He pulled Sally to the floor. She did not seem frightened.

"I'm used to this," she said flatly, her naked back and butt pushed against the metal frame of the bunk.

The Japs sprayed bullets wide. McLeane waited for them to stop and then crawled to the boxes that had served two years as a night table and got his automatic.

Great, he thought. I'm in the middle of the Pacific surrounded by Japs and have only a handgun and no pants. Half his tent had collapsed. At least the rumpled canvas provided some cover.

He knew the directions from which the shots had come, and he knew they had come from one, maybe two 8-mm Type 100 submachine guns. Other than that, he knew nothing.

In the lull he reached for his pants and threw Sally his shirt. She could cover some part of herself anyway.

"What do we do, Mack?"

"Something fast," he said, thinking while he talked.

213

He turned to Sally.

"When the fireworks start, get under that bunk."

"Great idea," she said, and meant it.

McLeane, primed like an animal, was on the balls of his feet and listening.

The fireworks would start soon, Sally thought, finishing the last button on his fatigue shirt.

Heinman had stepped outside to take in the moon.

"Ain't he romantic tonight," Wilkins said, no longer lying with his foot up. The bother of lying in traction hurt worse than the pain of an infected leg. He cut himself down. He didn't care how loudly the nurses would scream. His leg was his leg. The freedom allowed him to take his guns apart and clean them properly. Next to shooting, he liked cleaning his weapons more than anything in the world.

O'Connor had long since gone to sleep. He no longer let Wilkins' bedlamp or his talking keep him awake. In fact, unconsciously, he had learned how to retaliate with snores.

When Heinman came inside and walked over to his bunk, Wilkins knew that something was up. Heinman threw a pillow at O'Connor.

"We've got company," he said, picking up his automatic, shouldering his carbine, and attaching a couple of grenades to his belt.

Without any questions the other two Rangers moved like firemen at an alarm. Wilkins decided to fight the rest of the war in his underwear, grabbed his M-1 and his carbine, and hobbled after Heinman.

O'Connor, always a light sleeper who usually slept fully clothed, followed by a step.

They stood brazenly in the entrance to their quarters. The half-moon shed enough light to let them see the beach and across the water. They could sense shadows coming toward them like the fingers of a great monster.

Heinman and O'Connor spread out to cover the far flanks of the camp. Wilkins went inside to get a box on which he summarily sat and waited for the enemy to advance. Miffed did not describe his feelings. His going all over the Pacific to shoot Japs was one thing. Their coming to his backyard to shoot him was something else.

Heinman and O'Connor crawled along the sand in opposite directions. They wanted to get outside the Japs and drive them up the middle. Up the middle seems to be where the Japs wanted to go.

Suddenly, rushing low, the enemy opened fire and heaved grenades at the tents which, until minutes before, had housed the Rangers.

At the request of General MacArthur, General Thompson had left Vella la Vella to observe the combat on the Huon peninsula at the spot where Hill 457 once stood. So Flagg remained pretty much isolated in his quarters a half-mile from Ranger's camp. Except for Anna's visits no one came to see him. His wounds had almost healed, however, and he could get about himself. For the past two days he had felt well enough to have coffee at the canteen and to take his own meals. The rest of the time he read and slept.

The night of the attack found him dozing over his clipboard. He heard grenades go off but, at first, thought nothing of them. After all, that part of the Pacific was a war zone. Then again, the idea of grenades on Vella la Vella disturbed him. Why were grenades and Jap grenades at that exploding on Vella la Vella? He took his Thompson submachine gun and went outside.

He could not see much, even in the moonlight. The other camps were just too far away. Still, where the Rangers kept their tent, the sky did not look good. And he heard machinegun fire from that direction.

Flagg tried to still the panic in his stomach. He readjusted the glasses on his broken nose. He hoped they would stay put. He checked to see that he had ammo for his Thompson, a couple of grenades, his .45.

The longer he stood there the more sure he became of trouble everywhere. Flagg set out straight ahead. Maybe McLeane needed help.

Japanese Intelligence had assured Major Imamura that after the strike on Hill 457 the Rangers were completely demoralized. They were hurt badly and, if given time, would deteriorate even further. General Thompson, according to their sources, already had a new mission planned for them. The prospect of this new mission, plus their broken physical condition, had left the Rangers about to mutiny.

Japanese Intelligence had also assured Major Imamura that by waiting a week after the strike on Hill

457, various deployments would take the cadre normally billeted on Vella la Vella to the Huon peninsula to support MacArthur's troops.

Imamura took this intelligence the way he took all intelligence, with a grain of salt. He read the report, listened to the briefing, and figured reality would wait until he got there.

He would have to use intelligence reports of Vella la Vella's layout. He would have to assume that the Rangers lived where the Japanese high command said they lived. As for them being demoralized or the island being empty, he believed not one word of it. They would have to get in, hit, and get out fast.

Imamura planned to strike late at night when the Rangers were sleeping or very tired. He split his commandos according to their mission. He and Lieutenant Takata would take McLeane. Captain Iwabuchi and Corporal Anami had the task of blowing up the Catalina. Sergeant Nagasaki, Sergeants Tojo and Atsugi, and Private Kurito were left to destroy the rest of the Rangers. Captain Nara would fly them all in, dropping each in the water near his assignment and returing to join Iwabuchi and Anami in their demise of the Catalina.

That was how the Japanese strike force looked on paper.

The commandos had been excited the entire day of the attack. Each would outdo the other in feats of bravery. Each loved the Emperor and his country more. Each would bring untold honors to his family.

Imamura only hoped he had convinced them not

to die for their country, to make the other guy die for his. However, he feared that such hard Western thinking escaped them.

Nineteen

Corrigan had stopped screaming, Contardo noticed, though he couldn't see him.

Meanwhile, Contardo worked himself around almost 100 degrees to where he lay in shallow water, covered by areca palms, directly opposite the Catalina.

Anna fired an occasional round, but the Japs no longer fired back.

He could see two shadows hovering in the water behind the Catalina. If Anna was right and there was a third Jap, Contardo did not see him. He would have to take his chances. He would have to mess up whatever they were doing and mess *them* up right away.

He took off his boots, put his knife between his teeth, and slipped into the water. He would go out and come in behind the two Japs. They stood in shallow water. His problem would be keeping low enough.

The current offered no resistance and Contardo reached the men sooner than he expected.

Suddenly he struck two pair of legs. Startled, Anami fired his Nambu into the water, missing Contardo.

Contardo came up under the Japs, knocking the guns out of their hands. Anami fell back, but Iwabuchi grabbed Contardo by the throat. Contardo tossed the man off but the Jap only stumbled, regaining his footing in the surf.

He grabbed Contardo's legs and brought the prince of Flatbush down with him. Anami jumped on Contardo, and the two Japs held him under.

The emperor had not sent the usual goons, Contardo thought, holding his breath. These were very definitely specialists.

Contardo twisted and deftly worked himself out of their grip, but he had lost his knife. That put the Japs two knives and two guys ahead.

He wondered what had happened to Anna and to Corrigan, but not for long.

He did not have much time to wonder about anything. Anami and Iwabuchi had gathered strength and were both coming at him, each with a knife. Contardo backed up slowly, waiting for them to spring. They moved closer.

They went for his throat at once. Together they went into the air, one from the left and one from the right.

Contardo dropped to the ocean floor and, like lightning, came up behind them. He grabbed Iwabuchi in a hammerlock. Iwabuchi dropped his knife. Contardo used him as a shield. Anami would have to go around both of them to get at Contardo.

"Come on. Come and get me," Contardo chided as the two men circled with Iwabuchi in the middle. "Come on! Come on, go for it!"

Contardo bided his time.

"*AAAAAAHHHHHHHHIIIIIIIIEEEEEEEE.*"

Iwabuchi's scream tore apart the night.

Contardo had pushed Iwabuchi's arm up over his head, leaving it to dangle, broken, at his side. At the same time he kicked Anami in the groin hard enough to send him reeling backward into the water.

Contardo held him under with his foot while Iwabuchi, screaming about his arm, tried to grab at Contardo with whatever he could.

Contardo waited for him to come close enough and then let fly with a perfect right cross. He could feel Anami go limp under his foot. He then just picked the struggling Iwabuchi out of the water and with a quick snap of the hands, broke his neck.

The scream must have alerted another Jap. For the door of the Catalina flew open and Contardo could see, outlined against the light in the plane, the clear silhouette of a man in a wet suit.

The man shot, but well over his mark.

He's afraid, Contardo thought. He doesn't know who he'll hit.

Somehow, Contardo had to get him.

Again the figure came to the door of the plane. This time the bullets came seriously close to Contardo. Contardo hit the water. The figure gave another try. Then, suddenly, Contardo heard Corrigan's Owen and the figure fell from the Catalina into the water.

Contardo waded into shore, stopping by the body of the figure long enough to see that it was dead.

He dragged himself onto the beach, expecting to find Corrigan with his smart mouth and wondering what had happened to Anna.

Instead he found Anna, holding Corrigan's Owen and Corrigan sitting on a dendiki log, holding his head.

"What's goin' on here?" Contardo asked.

"Don't," Anna stopped Contardo. "He's very upset. The Catalina's left pontoon support has been severed, and the captain is taking it hard."

As Contardo got closer, he noticed Anna's uniform. She had been in the water. It dripped and hugged her body like skin. Even in the dim light of the moon he could see the outline of her breasts, the dark circle of her nipples. It occurred to Contardo that those who could think of pussy while being shot at would probably survive the war.

Corrigan tried to get up, but Anna went to him and gently set him down again.

"He has a head wound," she explained to Contardo. Contardo noticed that Corrigan didn't have a lot to say for once.

"He's still a little dazed."

"O.K. Take care of him . . . in a minute."

While Corrigan held his head and tried to keep from blanking out, Contardo pulled Anna to him, kissed her hard on the mouth and pressed his body close to hers. He could feel her breasts against his

222

chest, her belly against his loins, and he wanted her right then. Fuck the war.

"What is this shit?"

One grenade knocked Wilkins off his box, aggravating his leg but hurting only his pride. Just for effect he unloaded his carbine straight ahead of him.

"If you motherfuckers think I don't know how to use this thing, you had better think again."

Just after the four Jap commandos executed their plan to make a direct hit and go up the middle, they figured they had made a mistake. They had seen but one Ranger. An on the spot reassessment of the situation caused them to wonder where the others might be. Experience led them to believe that the rest be at their flank or even behind them.

Suddenly, the Japs felt trapped.

From the lull in the action, Heinman and O'Connor deduced the Japs were confused. They would be coming at him, Heinman thought. O'Connor wanted to drop a grenade on top of them.

Sergeants Atsugi and Nagasaki quickly deployed left and right. Serveant Tojo and Private Kurito continued the assault straight ahead, but slowly.

Heinman waited to see a dark figure come at him. O'Connor kept one hand on a grenade. He knew he could get them, even at forty yards once he could be sure of their positions.

The Rangers decided to let the Japs make the next move.

When coming up behind a target, military practice says as wide as possible. Atsugi and Nagasaki did not go wide enough and turned inside the two

Rangers. They did not realize what had happened until too late.

With the first move in the shadows Heinman knew what to do.

Nagasaki found himself in a death lock. Like an Indian, Heinman, grabbed him from behind in a fierce hammerlock. Nagasaki couldn't breathe. He clawed at Heinman's arm. He threw his arms backward around Heinman, but had no strength. He felt the life going out of his body. He tried to move his legs. Then with a quick snap Heinman broke his neck. The sound came like a twig breaking in the night.

O'Connor, not quite as lucky, was taken by surprise. The shadow he had been watching got the jump on him. He saw it come flying through the air at him. He lay there frozen for a second with a grenade in his hand. He spun away. A figure hit the ground three yards away. He found himself on the edge of a cluster of large brush. He threw the grenade on top of the figure ran like hell, and dove.

The explosion made his teeth hurt. He looked up to find a torn arm in front of him. He checked the damage. Cautiously, he put his hand on the motionless body. It felt like jello.

At the sound of the grenade Tojo and Kurito decided to die for the Emperor. They charged the tent, throwing grenades like rice at a wedding and screaming.

The grenades went over Wilkins' head, but the impact of so many of them managed to knock him down. He had no real idea which direction the attack had taken, who was coming at him from where or with what. He just lay down fire.

"Come and get it, you fuckers."

His carbine had run out of ammo. So had his Smith & Wesson, and he hit the ground. In that instant he saw a Jap grenade roll toward him. On pure reaction he picked it up and threw it. The grenade hit Sergeant Tojo square in the face. Wilkins heard the noise and looked up to see a headless body running toward him, the stump of a neck gushing blood. The body fell on him, flopped nervously, and died. Wilkins felt the ooze of human life flow down his own neck and back.

When he heard a carbine blast, he knew the Japs had been stopped.

Heinman had hit Kurito in the back, then he'd run in the dark, dust, and smoke to where Wilkins lay covered by Tojo. O'Connor also came running in from the far flank.

They both pulled Wilkins to his feet.

"How's the leg?" Heinman asked.

Wilkins hadn't thought about it.

"I don't know."

Even in the dark they could tell that the Japs had made a shambles of the tent. They wondered in silence what had happened to Contardo, McLeane, and Corrigan.

Flagg rubbed his hand on his fatigues. Sweat poured down his face and stung the wounds still open and raw. He blotted his eyes with his wrist. What was left of McLeane's tent lay just over the rise. He could hear Jap submachine-gun fire. He moved cautiously, but quickly. He got close. At least two Japs had McLeane pinned in cross fire.

Imamura and Takata fired at 130-degree angles to one another. McLeane could only retreat into a blind of torn and rumpled canvas. That, he decided, was the best way out or, always the aggressor, around.

"You'll be as safe under this bunk as anywhere," he told Sally, and disappeared beneath what used to be his roof.

McLeane and Flagg both misjudged. They came on the enemy sooner than expected. McLeane ran into Imamura on one side; Flagg caught Takata from the other way.

Both McLeane and Imamura, maneuvering for position, looked up in the dark brush to find each others' eyes. McLeane saw two slits in a wet suit staring at him. Imamura saw six feet of steel-hard, square-jawed American with a useless shoulder.

Something told McLeane he had just met the boss. Imamura knew exactly whom he had met. They hesitated, moved around each other. The situation did not call for guns. The two of them understood each other.

Imamura, charged with anticipation, wanted McLeane badly, wanted him for the Emperor, for himself. McLeane wanted to save his butt, first, and second, he wanted to teach the Japs the meaning of *no trespassing*.

Imamura threw a scissors around his knees and McLeane went to the ground. As he fell, McLeane drew his knife. Imamura fell on top of him, grabbed his wrist, gave him a knee in the groin.

McLeane wanted to wretch. For a moment he

could not see. Imamura had his knife. He felt the Jap's body on him. By instinct he moved. The hard blade missed him, barely. He still could not see. Imamura came at him again and again he twisted away and again Imamura struck and again he missed.

The two of them lay on the ground panting. Imamura decided the knife might not be the right weapon for killing McLeane, and he jumped at his throat.

McLeane felt the hands around his throat and the breath going out of him. He tried a knee to the groin. Imamura blocked it with his hip.

This guy moves like an eel, McLeane thought.

McLeane dug in with a heel and tried to move to the side, to power himself on top of the Jap. That didn't work either.

He put his hands between Imamura's arms, the ones that clung to his throat. He could not budge them. The Jap crushed McLeane's whole body.

McLeane had one breath left. He relaxed; Imamura hands loosened. McLeane planted his feet firmly in the ground and flipped the Jap hard over his own head. Imamura let out a yell and landed on his back.

They both struggled for the knife Imamura had dropped in the sand. McLeane came up with it. He lunged. Imamura jumped clear. McLeane grabbed him by the ankles, and the two tumbled on top of one enother.

Imamura kicked free, got up, and looked around.

On the ground, McLeane could hear an American carbine in the distance do its work. Three short definitive blasts meant a Jap had died somewhere.

Imamura knew it meant the same thing. From his left he could hear movement. Even if he couldn't see, he could feel an American coming in on his flank. Takata had been shot. He knew it somehow. Takata was dead. The other American came closer. McLeane went for Imamura, grabbed him by the back of his wet suit. Imamura fell. McLeane grabbed him by the shoulders. Imamura slipped away. The other American fired at Imamura's feet. Imamura broke free and ran, ran toward the beach. McLeane did not chase him. The bullets stopped hitting at the man's feet.

Imamura dived into the ocean and swam out to where Nara had hidden the plane. Major Imamura climbed in and flew off, depressed by defeat, happy to be alive.

On Vella la Vella Flagg and McLeane almost ran into each other.

"I almost had him," Flagg said.

McLeane looked up at the man for whom he had less use than any one in the military.

"But I got one back there," Flagg added.

McLeane got up. In silence the two men walked over to Takata's dead body.

Flagg seemed proud of himself. McLeane said nothing. He went back to where Sally waited for him.

Twenty

By the time the alarm sounded on Vella la Vella and by the time the main Marine force armed itself and figured out what was happening the Rangers had taken care of matters. As one radio corporal put it, on Vella la Vella no one expects anything unusual to happen. If something does happen, it has to be an air raid. Commandos aren't anywhere in the program. No one was looking for them.

Everyone on Vella la Vella, including the Rangers, had a chance to go over this in the hours after the attack. Marines on the island gathered in the canteen, laughed, and drank coffee and whatever else anyone could find.

Anna had a chance to explain what happened to her and Corrigan.

"One of the Japanese commandos wanted to get on board the Catalina," she said at the table while everyone listened. "The captain went wild."

Corrigan nodded his head, but said nothing.

"The captain just kept firing and firing. The commando came up on the other side of the plane, shot at the captain, and thought he had killed him because the captain fell in the water.

"But the commando only grazed the captain's head. He climbed on board the Catalina. I pulled the captain out of the ocean together with his submachine gun.

"When the commando stuck his head out of the Catalina again, I was able to pick him off. It's really that simple. Meanwhile, the captain here feels pretty good, don't you, captain?"

In fact, Corrigan felt moderately satisfactory. His head hurt. His plane had been damaged. His self-esteem had not been enhanced either.

Contardo looked across the table at Anna. In the light of the canteen she was beautiful even with her hair disheveled and her dress rumpled. He felt proud of her. For the first time in his life he felt proud of a woman.

Sally eyed McLeane. She wanted to snuggle against his strong chest. As for McLeane, the pain in his shoulder had become unbearable, but he said nothing.

He glanced around at his men. They seemed to be in good shape. He wanted to send Wilkins to Sydney to get his leg checked by some top flight doctors. He would have to knock out Wilkins first, he knew, to get him there.

Everyone laughed and relived the details of the attack until the wee hours of the morning. Then, suddenly tired, the meeting broke up so they all could get some sleep. Anna and Sally decided to put up at the BOQ for women which remained intact. Corrigan insisted on returning to the Catalina.

On the way out McLeane stopped Flagg.

"Major," he said. "I owe you one."

"No you don't. Let's just say we're even."

The two men shook hands.

"Thanks," McLeane added.

They parted. McLeane turned and signaled Flagg thumbs up. Flagg smiled and waved.

Back at the remains of his quarters McLeane met with a surprise in the person of Margot Thomas. A seaplane had just left her on the beach. She stood with her duffle bag in front of the collapsed tent. She did not run to greet him.

His shoulder hurt too much to hold her or put his arm around her.

"She must have been a real tigress in bed," Margot said, looking alternately at the wreckage and at Sally, who stood a discreet distance away.

McLeane was too smart to ask how Margot had learned about Sally. He kept his mouth shut.

Margot planned to sleep at the women's enlisted quarters for the night—maybe forever. She picked up her bag and walked to the radio center. McLeane wanted to help her.

"Stop," Sally said. "She's mad at you now, Major. After all, she's your girl. She still may want your services tonight."

McLeane watched Margot disappear over the

rise. With one good arm he set to straightening out his tent at least enough so he could sleep.

Wilkins, sitting on boxes and still in his underwear, barked out orders while Heinman, O'Connor, and Contardo rearranged their own sleeping quarters.

"I swear you guys are slow." Wilkins shook his head. "I could have those two girls do it faster than you."

Those two girls referred to Anna and Sally. Contardo was not sure he liked the reference.

After an hour they had made some headway. One side of the tent stood relatively straight. Wilkins' banter however, did not let up.

"Can we get this here thing a little more vertical? We don't want sloppy work around here."

A few more minutes of Wilkins and the Rangers dropped their work. They knew what they had to do. With great purpose they walked straight to where he sat like a slave lord, with his M-1 across his lap and his leg up, and carefully, but deliberately picked him up.

"Put me down," Wilkins said.

The Rangers nodded among themselves.

"Be careful of my leg."

They walked to the lagoon and threw him in. Then they carried him to a clump of bushes yards from where they were working and placed him in the sand with his back to them so he could not see what they did.

"Now you can give all the orders you want," O'Connor said, patting Wilkins on the head. "Talk to the fish.''

"I'll get you guys for this," he screamed as they walked away.

"And don't go nowhere," added Contardo.

"My leg! My leg!"

"Fuck your leg!" Contardo yelled back.

He had no sooner said that than he saw Anna coming toward him. He went to meet her.

"Hi, my hero." She put her arms around him. Being her hero made Contardo feel good.

In the background he could hear Wilkins' voice, but not a word of what he said. He and Anna walked away from the camp. He had his arm around her. She slowed down and then turned.

"We're leaving, Vince,"

He could not remember if she'd ever called him by his first name before. He just nodded his head.

"General Thompson has orders for us. We're shipping out for Darwin. There's a hospital there and the duty should be good."

"What's he doing here? I thought he was off watching the war with MacArthur."

"He's here. Make no mistake about that. And so's McLeane's girl friend."

"Margot?"

"How many's he got?"

They stood close, but did not touch.

"When do you leave?"

"The engines are going on the plane."

"I'll walk you over."

Contardo had a momentary sick feeling in the pit of his stomach, but he shook that. Nothing could last. It had to end sooner or later. He squeezed her as they walked. Besides, what's another broad? Flatbush has lots of broads, and he would be back there soon. Or maybe he wouldn't. It didn't make any difference.

A seaplane smaller than the Catalina waited off shore. Sally stood alone against the horizon with two bags at her feet.

"I guess Mack couldn't make it."

"He doesn't know. Sally didn't want to say goodbye. It's better that way."

"Yeah, it's better."

She reached up and kissed Contardo softly on the lips.

"You're wonderful Vince, and I'll always love you."

Protestations of love always made Contardo uneasy.

"Something like that," he said looking away.

Neither of them spoke.

"Look, I've got to get back to the guys. You take it easy, and I'll see you around."

Without further hesitation he turned and headed back from the direction he'd come.

"Remember, I'll always love you," Anna called after him.

Contardo didn't say anything, but he gave her McLeane's old thumbs-up sign and kept right on going.

By the end of the evening life on Vella la Vella had returned to a relatively normal state. All tents had been erected again. Most of the Rangers had gotten some kind of sleep. Heinman had lost himself in the latest anthropological journal. O'Connor had a new idea for a bomb. Wilkins had decided to abandon supervision for cleaning guns, something he did better and enjoyed more. Only Contardo behaved a little oddly. Instead of abusing everyone with his mouth he preferred to walk alone along the beach. The other Rangers wondered how long that would last.

General Thompson sat at the canteen with Flagg, hatching plans. Intelligence may not be perfect, insisted Flagg, but any information was always better than no information at all, a bit of thinking McLeane would have found highly arguable. Thompson felt proud of the Rangers and proud, too, that he could always place them at the disposal of Comsopac. When the war was over, finally, they would have played a great part in bringing it to a just end. Sometimes, even over coffee, Thompson got carried away. Anyway, for a while, his stomach hadn't bothered him, and that had to be a good sign.

As for McLeane, Margot's anger had turned back to hurt. She had decided to speak to him again. She even put a new dressing on his shoulder.

"I know she's a nurse, Mack, but was she as gentle as I am?"

She very carefully swabbed McLeane's open would with warm water.

"No, Margot, she was not as gentle as you are."

She let her fingers wander over his chest.

"Are you sure?"

"Yes, I'm sure."

Her hands moved lower, to his stomach.

"Are you still sure?"

"I am still sure."

She pushed McLeane back onto the pillows and sat down beside him on the bed. She loosened his belt and undid his pants. Her hands massaged around his groin, touching, occasionally, the end of his cock, the underside of his balls.

"Are you absolutely positive?"

He nodded.

She leaned over and put the end of his organ in her mouth, nipping it lightly with her teeth. With her free hand she undid her shirt to expose her naked breasts.

"And her breasts? Were her breasts as nice as these?" She took them in her hands and held them up.

He shook his head, then lowered it and sucked on the nipples.

"Definitely not as nice."

He grabbed Margot and pulled her to him.

"I love you so much, Mack," she said into his chest. "Why do you do these things?"

When he did not answer she decided not to press him. He undressed her quickly and loved her hard and long.

Major Imamura spent a less happy evening. When General Sasaki saw him return alone, he spit all over himself.

"Wait! Wait right here!" the general screamed without any inscrutability at all. Imamura stood in the outer chamber of the general's bamboo hideaway still wearing his wet suit.

He stood for hours.

236

The general came back, apparently calm, and proceeded to give Imamura an account of what had happened. In every detail that Imamura could himself verify the general was correct. Intelligence did a great job of gathering information after the fact. Before the fact they do not do so well, he thought to himself.

He stood at attention while the general went on and on, but he did not listen. He knew his mistakes. He knew how many men he'd lost. He knew he would never speak English again with Lieutenant Takata. He also knew how tough the Rangers were and had a better idea of what it would take to get them next time.

"And why didn't you die?"

The general screamed the question.

"Too many years at Princeton," he blurted. The answer just came out. He did not mean to be insubordinate. He did not want to lie either.

The general did not understand, but dismissed Imamura in disgust.

Walking back to the camp that had been the home of the commandos for so many weeks, he felt sad, then angry. He wanted to break something. Instead he pulled his automatic to fire into the nearest tree. The Nambu jammed. He threw it away and walked into his tent.

He would kill McLeane and the Rangers. Given one more chance he would get them.

THE SURVIVALIST SERIES
by Jerry Ahern

#1: TOTAL WAR   (960, $2.50)
The first in the shocking series that follows the unrelenting search
for ex-CIA covert operations officer John Thomas Rourke to locate
his missing family—after the button is pressed, the missiles
launched and the multimegaton bombs unleashed . . .

#2: THE NIGHTMARE BEGINS   (810, $2.50)
After WW III, the United States is just a memory. But ex-CIA
covert operations officer Rourke hasn't forgotten his family. While
hiding from the Soviet forces, he adheres to his search!

#3: THE QUEST   (851, $2.50)
Not even a deadly game of intrigue within the Soviet High Command, and a highly placed traitor in the U.S. government can
deter Rourke from continuing his desperate search for his family.

#4: THE DOOMSAYER   (893, $2.50)
The most massive earthquake in history is only hours away, and
Communist-Cuban troops, Soviet-Cuban rivalry, and a traitor in
the inner circle of U.S. II block Rourke's path.

#5: THE WEB   (1145, $2.50)
Blizzards rage around Rourke as he picks up the trail of his family
and is forced to take shelter in a strangely quiet Tennessee valley
town. But the quiet isn't going to last for long!

#6: THE SAVAGE HORDE   (1243, $2.50)
Rourke's search for his wife and family gets sidetracked when he's
forced to help a military unit locate a cache of eighty megaton war-
head missiles. But the weapons are hidden on the New West
Coast—and the only way of getting to them is by submarine!

*Available wherever paperbacks are sold, or order direct from the
Publisher. Send cover price plus 50¢ per copy for mailing and han-
dling to Zebra Books, 475 Park Avenue South, New York, N.Y.
10016. DO NOT SEND CASH.*